An uplifting story of friendship and hope

Can Joe find the courage he needs?

Get swept up in the beauty and wildness of the moorlands

Tackling contemporary issues, can we save the hen harriers?

Perfect for fans of Michael Morpurgo and Laurent St John

'*Sky Dancer* addresses the important and urgent issue of the conflict between protecting and exploiting the environment. The book is filled with vivid and beautiful descriptions of every place that the story visits; I especially enjoyed the portrayal of the moor. The writing gave me such a "birds eye view" that I felt I too was really there.'

Saffron

'This is yet another amazing book that Gill Lewis has written. I was hooked from beginning to end in a whirlwind of emotions. It was like the words were a painting, each a specific colour dancing off the page, each sentence painting thousands of pictures.'

Charlotte

'Quietly gripping with a thought-provoking ending, clever in the way it asks lots of interesting questions of the reader as well as of the characters themselves.'

Felix

'*Sky Dancer* starts amazing and keeps on getting better. I was gripped by the story. I learned so much about birds and how they live on grouse moors. I loved this story and will recommend it to all my class and everyone who loves animal stories.'

Cecily

For the Wild Things

OXFORD
UNIVERSITY PRESS

Great Clarendon Street, Oxford OX2 6DP

Oxford University Press is a department of the University of Oxford.
It furthers the University's objective of excellence in research, scholarship,
and education by publishing worldwide. Oxford is a registered trade mark of
Oxford University Press in the UK and in certain other countries

Copyright © Gill Lewis 2017

Inside illustrations copyright © Gelrev Ongbico 2017

The moral rights of the author have been asserted

Database right Oxford University Press (maker)

First published 2017

British Library Cataloguing in Publication Data

Data available

ISBN: 978-0-19-274925-3

1 3 5 7 9 10 8 6 4 2

Printed in Great Britain by Clays Ltd, St Ives plc

Paper used in the production of this book is a natural,
recyclable product made from wood grown in sustainable forests.
The manufacturing process conforms to the environmental
regulations of the country of origin.

Sky Dancer

GILL LEWIS

OXFORD
UNIVERSITY PRESS

CHAPTER 1

I'm a coward.

There, I've said it now.

I'm a coward.

It's true.

Dad never actually said it out loud, but it was always in his eyes.

He would've known that I wouldn't go to his funeral and that I'd sit in the car instead, slumped low so nobody could see me.

He would've known that I wouldn't want to be the one to scatter his ashes too.

I just don't want to do it.

I don't want to even think about it.

I want to stay here at home until it's all over, but Mum and Ryan say I have to scatter his ashes. I have to say goodbye. They say I'll regret it if I don't.

I even looked up cremation on the Internet to see what human ashes look like.

You find some weird stuff on the Internet.

In 1907 Dr Duncan MacDougall carried out an experiment to prove that the human soul has weight. He discovered that the average human soul weighs 21 grams. Turns out, it was a rubbish experiment and he only recorded the results he wanted to find. Still, it makes you think doesn't it? Dad's ashes weigh three kilograms, as much as three bags of sugar and that's a lot by human standards, at least that's what Mr Arkwright, the funeral director said. But it doesn't seem much, not compared to the size Dad was in life. Mr Arkwright said the ashes are just our bones, mainly. The rest, the soft bits, the muscle and fat and all our insides, burn and turn into steam and smoke. Just the bones left, burnt and crushed into ashes. Sometimes there are tooth fillings, bits of jewellery and artificial hips and stuff, but Dad didn't have any of those. Still, it makes you wonder doesn't it? What makes us, *us*? What is the soul anyway? Is it something flapping angels hand out when we enter this earth, or just electricity in our head that flicks out like a light bulb when we die?

I stare at the back of Ryan striding ahead of me, the stretched canvas of his gamekeeper's bag outlining the pine casket holding Dad's ashes.

Dad's bones.

Ryan's like a clone of Dad. He's only eighteen but he's six feet tall, and built like the massive gritstone slabs that shape this landscape. I reckon Ryan's ashes would weigh the same as Dad's. Mine would weigh less than half, I'm sure. I'm six years younger than Ryan, but I'll never be as big as him. I'm stick-thin and short. Like Mum.

I fall in behind Ryan, trying to follow his path. It's not quite dawn, and the moors lie dark and silent, stretched out before us. Above, heavy clouds slide across the sky, like the hulls of vast ships passing overhead. It's cold too. A skittish wind whips through the heather and stings the back of my neck. I pull my collar higher and wish I'd grabbed my thicker coat. It's nearly the end of June but it feels more like winter.

Ahead of Ryan, two birds explode from the cover of heather, their wings whirring away downwind. Even in this light I can see they are a pair of red grouse, their dark shapes streaking away, hugging the contours of the moor.

Ryan spins around. His face is hidden in shadow, but I don't have to see it, to know he's mad at me.

'Joe, keep your bloody dog under control.'

I can see Weasel bouncing after the birds, jumping up in the air, her long ears flapping as if she's trying to take off after them.

'Weasel!' I yell. She doesn't hear, or at least pretends

not to. 'WEASEL!' I yell again. I whistle several times and she gives up the chase, bounding back to me.

Ryan scowls, hunches his shoulders against the wind, and sets off again. His own dog, Teal, and Dad's old dog, Widgeon, trot by his side.

'Heel, Weasel,' I whisper. I click my fingers for her to walk beside me and she wags her long tail and licks my hand. I don't want to give Ryan any more excuses to get rid of her. She's a springer spaniel, but not working stock. She's chunkier than the working dogs and her tail's been left undocked. I got her free from a townie who couldn't keep her and wanted her put down. She had torn up his house and dug up the garden when she was left alone. All she needed was some exercise but Ryan's got no time for her. She's too soft, a lapdog, he says. She'll chase the birds if she's got half a chance. Worst of all she's gun-shy. She runs a mile at the sound of a single shot.

As we climb the moor, Black Rock rises up above us. The slabs of dark gritstone at its peak are silhouetted against the paling sky.

It's where we're heading.

Black Rock was Dad's favourite place. It sits high in the south Pennines, on the moorland roof of England. He used to say you could see the whole world from there. When I was little, I thought I'd be able to see China and Australia and America. But I think what Dad meant was that he could see *his* whole world from there . . . across the whole Hartstone estate, down into its valleys and wooded cloughs, and to Hartstone Hall, the dark stone mansion with its walled gardens and cobblestone courtyard and stables. Hartstone is the home of Henry Knight, the owner of this moor.

Ryan scrambles up on to the top and stands facing the wind. On the eastern horizon, the sun breaks through a gap in the cloud, its golden light setting fire to the tips of the heather.

I breathe in the moor . . . the damp peat, the heather, and the smell of fresh rain on the earth.

I look at the place Dad always sat, a natural stone seat sheltered by the rock. Dad would settle himself in the shadow of Black Rock, take a swig of whisky from his hip flask, and survey the moor. Dad was the head gamekeeper for Hartstone Moor, like his father and grandfather before him.

Gamekeeping was in his blood.

In his soul.

Ryan's looking at the empty seat too. He places his shotgun and bag on the ground beside him and takes a swig from the hip flask in his pocket. Dad's shotgun, Dad's hip flask. Ryan claimed them as his right. All I have is Dad's old pair of binoculars. They're army issue and the weight of a brick.

Ryan reaches into his bag and pulls out the pine casket.

His knuckles are white as he grips its edges and I can see his hands shake. He pulls the lid and I stare at the powder of Dad's bones. There are dark, gritty, charcoal-like lumps amongst finer ash, which is a pale smoke-grey.

'Let's do it then,' says Ryan.

I nod my head but we both just stand there, neither of us knowing what to do next.

Ryan reaches in and scoops a handful of Dad's ashes. He stares at them, frowning as if he's trying to read words in the ash.

'Ashes to ashes,' he says.

His voice falters. The words feel out of place. Borrowed from a church. A formality. They're the kind of thing you're meant to say, but they don't sound right here. Maybe the wind hissing through the heather and the haunting dawn call of a curlew are words enough for Dad. Ryan throws the handful of ash into the air. The dark, gritty pieces fall to the ground, but the wind snatches the finer flecks of pale ash and carries them high across the heather.

I watch Dad returning to the moor to become the peat and the heather, and to flow in its streams and rivers. I watch the landscape that created him, taking him back.

Ryan holds out the casket to me. 'Your turn.'

I look at the gritty ash and shake my head. 'It's OK. You do it.'

Ryan spits on the ground. 'Don't be a wimp, Joe. Do it. Do it for Dad.'

I don't want to touch Dad's ashes. I shake my head and fold my arms, pressing my hands against my sides.

'Do it,' orders Ryan, shoving the casket against my chest.

I hesitate, then lift my hand, my fingers hovering over the casket.

'C'mon,' says Ryan. 'Do it now.'

I grab a handful and fling it up into the air, keen to let go. A gust of wind whips past and snatches Dad's ashes high into the sky. The gritty pieces fall to earth, but I watch the fine white ash drift slowly down towards the valley, a pale ghost of Dad riding the wind, skimming the heather.

Then I see another ghost rise up to meet him.

Pale smoke-grey, it glides across the moor on broad outstretched wings tipped with black. It's a bird of prey. A male hen harrier. A sky dancer.

It dips back down and quarters low over the heather, switching this way and that.

It's so strange that we should see it now, at this moment.

I hope Ryan hasn't seen, but Ryan's like Dad. He never misses anything.

'Bloody bird.' Ryan curses beneath his breath.

It's not until I hear the click of barrels close on the stock of the shotgun, that I realize Ryan's loaded up and taking aim.

I hold my breath, hoping the bird will glide out of sight, but he flies closer, moving back and forth, his attention directed to the heather.

'Don't, Ryan,' I whisper. I can feel my heart thump against my chest. 'Don't! There'll be Birders watching somewhere. You'll get caught, like Dad.'

'Bloody bird.' He narrows his eye. 'I owe Dad this.'

I sense him find the bird in his line of sight and track it across the moor. His finger slides towards the trigger. I can't let him do this. I can't.

I reach up and yank his sleeve.

Ryan spins around. 'What the hell d'you do that for?'

'Don't,' I say. 'Adam Thorne might be out there with his camera again.'

Ryan glares at me. 'D'you think I care? He as good as killed Dad.'

'He'd love nothing better than to get you put in prison too.'

Ryan pulls his arm away. 'Like I said. I don't care.'

He puts the shotgun to his shoulder again, but the bird has disappeared into the soft folds of shadow. 'You should've let me shoot it.'

'Let it go, Ryan. Dad's gone. It's over.'

Ryan grabs my coat so fast that I can't back away. He hauls me up, and I feel my heels come off the ground. His voice is cold and he almost spits the words in a harsh whisper. 'It's not over. Not for me. Not for you. Going to prison gave Dad his heart attack, that's what the doctors said. Prison killed him.'

I try and push him off, but Ryan's grip is like iron. 'Dad broke the law,' I say. 'You know that. Adam Thorne filmed him shooting that hen harrier. He had proof.'

Ryan pulls me even closer so our faces are almost touching. 'You just don't get it do you? Dad said you were soft in the head like them Birders. He said you'd never make a gamekeeper. You don't have it in you.'

My throat feels tight and it's not just Ryan's hand pressing against my neck that's making it hard to breathe. His words are like a punch in the chest. I try and push him off. 'Gerroff,' I splutter.

Ryan lets go of me. 'Dad loved this moor, Joe. Never forget that. He gave his life protecting it.' He picks up the casket and walks away to stand with his back to me. He doesn't include me this time. Instead he scoops handfuls of Dad's ashes and casts them into the wind with fast, angry swipes. I watch the ash spiral away across the heather. When he's done, Ryan spins around, picks up his gun and marches past without looking at me, his face hard, like rock.

I watch Ryan stride away. This isn't how it's meant to be. I try to force myself to cry; to feel something, anything. I try to think of a happy time, something Dad and I did together. But the truth is I don't feel anything at all. I don't think Dad loved me.

I was never good enough for him.

I'm too soft.

Too scared.

Too small.

I let Dad down.

And now I'll never be able to make it right with him, and it hangs like a heavy weight around my soul.

CHAPTER 2

I follow Ryan home, keeping my distance from him as we leave the open moorland and pick our way down the steep-sided valley. Trees dig their roots into the shallow soil. Spindly birches cling to the higher ground while gnarled oaks, green and furred with moss, interlock their roots around boulders on the lower slopes. It's warmer here, sheltered. Fine mist hangs like breath in the still air.

Hartstone Brook tumbles down through this clough to merge and join with all the other brooks to become the wide meandering river, which slides away across the lowland valley through the towns and distant cities and eventually to the sea. In this blue dawn, the soft folds of landscape are still wrapped in the shadow of night. From up here, the lights of towns and villages cluster like a small galaxies of stars in the darkness. And it feels as if I'm floating through the vast emptiness of space, between different worlds. I want to hold on to Ryan and keep him close, but he, like the stars, seems so far away and unreachable.

Weasel is somewhere in the undergrowth searching for rabbits. I catch glimpses of the top of her tail zigzagging above the bracken. She disappears for a moment, but the alarm call of a startled blackbird gives her away.

'Weasel!' I yell. 'WEASEL!'

She comes bounding back to me, wearing her happy face, tongue lolling. Spiky baubles of burdock seeds hook into the long fur of her ears and tail, and I curse inwardly knowing it'll take ages to pull them all out.

At the bottom of the valley, I cross the small footbridge to feel the sun on my face, while Ryan sticks to the side of the valley in shadow.

And we walk like that, on opposite sides of the brook, the rushing water filling our silence with its noise, neither of us looking at the other.

We head home down towards the two gamekeepers' cottages huddled against the hillside. The early morning sun has brought colour back into the world, lifting the softness of the moor. A low stone wall borders our garden, keeping the moorland edge at bay. The manicured lawn and flowerbeds are Mum's attempt at keeping order in the wilderness.

A light shines from our cottage and I can see Mum inside the kitchen washing dishes at the sink. She must be back from her night shift at the care home. I march ahead of Ryan, leaving him to put his dogs back in their kennels and feed his ferrets.

Mum turns around when I open the door. 'Where's Ryan?'

'Outside,' I say. I grab a bit of toast from the table.

'Wash your hands first,' says Mum. She glances down at Weasel, at the muddy trail of paw prints circling the kitchen floor. 'And how many times have I told you to put her in the kennel or wipe her feet?'

'Sorry,' I mutter. I grab a dog towel and start rubbing Weasel's paws.

Mum sits down at the table and pours a cup of tea. 'I'm sorry, love,' she says. 'Didn't mean to snap. I'm just a bit tired, that's all.'

I sit next to her and Weasel puts a paw on Mum's knee, eyeing the toast on the table.

Mum softens and pulls a corner of toast to feed her. 'And don't let Ryan see me do this,' she says to her. 'He says you're too soft already.'

'How's Nan?' I say, although I already know Mum's answer to my question.

'Same,' says Mum.

Nan's lived at the care home where Mum works since

Gramps died. She doesn't recognize Ryan or me anymore. She remembers the long distant past as if it was yesterday, and doesn't remember yesterday at all. She only asks after Dad, but Mum hasn't got the heart to tell her every day that her son has died.

Weasel slides under the table when Ryan walks in. He hangs his bag on the back of the door, lays his shotgun on the pine dresser and washes his hands.

'I've got cooked breakfast for the both of you,' says Mum, pulling two plates out of the oven. 'Thought you'd need it.'

'Thanks, Mum,' I say. I squeeze a splodge of tomato sauce next to my bacon.

I can see mum eyeing the pine casket in Ryan's bag. She didn't come with us to scatter Dad's ashes. She said it was father and son stuff. Truth is, in all those years, she hardly ever came out on the moor. It was Dad's place, somehow. She was never part of it.

Mum looks at me then at Ryan. 'You did it then?'

Ryan nods.

'On Black Rock?' says Mum.

Ryan nods again, and walks with his shotgun into the boot room. I hear his keys unlock the gun cupboard to put the gun away.

Mum looks at me. 'Is he OK?' she whispers.

I stab a sausage. 'We saw a hen harrier. A male one.'

Mum takes a sip of tea, but her eyes don't leave me. 'What did Ryan do?'

'What d'you think?'

Mum takes a deep sigh and breathes out slowly.

'I stopped him,' I say. 'He'll shoot it next time. I know he will.'

I can hear Ryan coming back into the kitchen. I stuff the sausage in my mouth, lean forward and put my elbow on the table so I don't have to look at him. We eat in silence, our knives and forks clattering on the plates.

Mum boils up the kettle for another pot of tea. 'We're going to have new neighbours,' she says. 'That'll be nice won't it?'

'Who's coming?' I ask. The cottage next to us has been empty for over two years since Nan went into the care home. It belongs to the Hartstone Estate too. It's in a worse state than ours. At least our heating is working.

'A new teacher for your old primary school apparently,' says Mum. 'She's going to rent it over the summer.'

Ryan scowls. 'Let's hope the leaky roof puts her off.'

Mum sits back and sips her tea. 'It'll be nice to have neighbours for a change. It's a bit lonely up here.'

Ryan wipes a piece of bread around his plate, soaking up spilled egg yolk. He couldn't frown more if he tried. 'We don't need neighbours. It's fine how it is.'

Mum sighs. 'I'm off to bed for a few hours. I'm working at the Bird in Hand this evening and it's always busy on a Saturday night. There's pizza in the freezer for both of you tonight.'

I glance at Mum. She's taken on more jobs since Dad died. Still, we're lucky that Henry Knight took Ryan on as assistant gamekeeper and let us keep renting the cottage.

She sees me looking. 'What are you both up to today?'

Ryan gets up and shoves his plate in the dishwasher. 'I'll be out all day. We're counting the grouse, getting estimates for the shooting season.'

'So I hear Jolly Jackson is in charge now?' says Mum.

Ryan mutters something under his breath, pulls on his coat and leaves the kitchen.

Jolly Jackson is the new head gamekeeper. He was Dad's assistant and Ryan can't stand him.

'What about you?' says Mum with false brightness in her voice. 'Are you playing football today?'

I shake my head. 'Match is cancelled. I might meet Luke and the others in the park.'

Mum stifles a yawn. 'D'you need a lift?'

'It's OK,' I say. She looks dog-tired. 'I'll walk and get the bus at the bottom of the hill. You get some sleep.'

Weasel follows me out into the back yard and slinks into the kennel with her tail down when I open the door.

'You've had a walk,' I say, pushing the bolt across. 'I'll be back later.' She just stares up at me with her big eyes and I feel like a traitor leaving her there. But I want to see Luke and Billy and kick a football around in the park. It's where normal is. I actually wish it wasn't Saturday. I'd rather be with my mates at school, away from Ryan walking around with a great cloud hanging over him, and Mum trying to keep us both happy, but rushing between several jobs and with never enough time to be here for us.

I don't want it to be like this.

But I don't want it to be like it was before either.

I look down the long garden, beyond the cage with Ryan's ferrets, to Dad's work shed at the end. I haven't been in there since he died. It's got all his gamekeeping stuff; his set of tools, immaculately oiled and looked after, the fox snares and tunnel traps and coils of wire and fencing. I couldn't go in if I wanted to. Ryan's locked the door and kept the key. He won't go in there himself either, but it's as if he's claimed Dad for his own, locked himself up inside his memories and won't let any of us in.

I go up to my room and stuff my phone in my pocket, grab some change, and pull on my old trainers. Outside, the clouds have broken up, opening patches of blue. A stiff breeze bends the tops of the conifers that shield our cottage from the winds that can tear across these moors. I don't reckon it will rain, so I pull on my hoodie and head back downstairs and out of the door.

'Joe, are you still here?'

I stick my head around the kitchen door. 'Just off,' I say.

Mum's wrapped up in her dressing gown. 'Ryan's forgotten his lunch and I've money for the rent,' she says waving an envelope in her hand. 'It's a month late. I wanted him to take it to Hartstone Hall.'

'Give him a ring,' I say. 'Get him to come back.'

'I've tried. His phone must be off or he's out of signal.' Mum tips her head to the side. 'You wouldn't see if you could catch him up would you?'

'He'll be half a mile away by now,' I say. 'It's his fault he forgot his lunch.'

Mum tries to wipe the tiredness from her eyes. 'I'll get changed again and nip over there now in the car,' she sighs. 'Don't be hard on him, Joe. This isn't easy for any of us.'

I snatch the envelope with the money and Ryan's lunch too. 'I'll go,' I snap. I'm only doing it to help Mum. If it weren't for paying the rent money, I wouldn't bother. I don't care if Ryan goes hungry. I couldn't care less.

CHAPTER 3

I let Weasel out again and she bounds around me as if I've been away for a week. I ruffle the fur on her head. 'Come on, daft dog.' We head out south along the Hare's track, which runs along the bottom of Hare's Leap Hill. The track is overgrown, and eroded where water from the hills has scooped out deep gullies, but it's the quickest way on foot from here to Hartstone Hall. It's about two miles, and if I keep up the pace I'll be able to get back to town in time to meet Luke and Billy in the park.

Besides, I don't mind the walk. The wide skies give me headspace to think, away from home and school.

The moorland slopes uphill, a patchwork pattern of vivid greens and strips of reddish heather. Weasel bounds ahead of me, setting up a pair of red grouse and they whirr away, streaking low, uttering their alarm call, '*Go-*

back . . . go-back . . . go-back . . .'. Their russet feathers shine almost bronze in the morning light.

Hartstone is one of the oldest grouse moors in England. Even now it feels like it is a step back into the past. According to the Knight family, driven grouse shooting really took off right here. It's a story I've heard Henry Knight tell a thousand times to shooting guests. Over a hundred and fifty years ago, Sir William Knight discovered he could kill loads of grouse if he hid in a ditch and waited for a line of people to scare the birds and drive them towards him. Apparently when Queen Victoria visited, she was so impressed by the huge numbers of grouse shot in this way that she did the same at Balmoral, her estate in Scotland. Estates all over the country took up driven grouse shooting after that, but Henry Knight says it all began here, at Hartstone Moor. It's still known as the best grouse moor in England and Henry Knight wants to keep it that way.

In just over a month's time the moor will be alive with gunfire at the start of the grouse-shooting season.

Grouse shooting begins on the twelfth of August.

The Glorious Twelfth.

The Guns and the loaders will be hunkered down in the shooting butts, the circular stone shelters camouflaged on the moor, where they'll be waiting for the beaters to drive the grouse forward.

And there's nothing like it, with the smell of gunpowder and the grouse streaking like arrows overhead. It's one big party. And the best bit is that I get paid fifty quid for just walking across the moor in a line with other beaters, waving a white flag to scare the grouse and drive them forward to fly to the Guns.

The twelfth of August was the most important date in Dad's calendar; more important than Christmas, or New Year, or even our birthdays. It was everything Dad worked for, to look after the moors and keep the grouse numbers high for the next shooting season. Now the moors seem empty without him.

I don't catch up with Ryan until I reach Hartstone Hall. I enter the stable yard and see Ryan sitting on a mounting block outside Dad's old office. Jolly Jackson is inside, at the desk where Dad used to sit, typing at the computer.

'Mum sent me with your lunch,' I say to Ryan, holding out the lunchbox with his sandwiches.

Ryan takes them from me without even looking up.

'You could say thank you,' I snap. 'I'm missing football cos of you.'

Ryan doesn't say anything. He shoves the sandwiches in his keeper's bag and stares ahead. Behind me I hear the office door click open.

'Hello, Joe! Good to see you.'

I look round to see Jolly Jackson at the door. He's short and stocky with ruddy cheeks and a thatch of yellow hair. His usual jovial smile looks forced today.

Jolly pulls on his tweed jacket. 'It's good to have you both back on the moor. It's going to be a busy season.'

I hear Ryan muttering something beneath his breath. I'm sure Jolly's heard too, but if he did, he doesn't show it.

'It's a good grouse year,' I say, trying to make up for Ryan's silence.

Jolly nods enthusiastically. 'It is. One of the best for a while. It's been a dry spring and so lots of chicks survived this year.'

Ryan pulls a dandelion from a crack in the stonework and shreds it between his fingers. 'It's a good grouse year because Dad did his job right.'

'Yes, indeed,' Jolly nods vigorously. 'And I hope we can keep up his good work. He taps his walking stick on the ground and turns to me. 'Are you coming to join us counting grouse today? We could do with some help.'

I shake my head. 'Mum sent me to bring the rent money. It's a bit late, sorry.'

Jolly gives me a pat on the shoulder. 'Well I hope you can join us another day.'

I think he means it too. It's going to be a long day for him on the moor with just Ryan for company.

'Go in and give the money to Patricia,' Jolly says, waving his stick at Hartstone Hall. 'She's in Henry's office.'

I leave my trainers by the back entrance and tell Weasel to wait as I enter the house past the boot room. Estelle, the housekeeper nods her head at me. I haven't been back here since Dad died, and it feels strange somehow. I don't often come into the house, but it hasn't changed. It's dark inside and silent. The Knight family live in the west wing for most of the year, only using the rest of the house when guests stay. I make my way up the back stairs into the corridor behind the great hall. Different members of the Knight family, past and present, stare down at me from their portraits hanging on the wooden panelled walls. The house smells of beeswax and lemon floor polish. I pause at the open door of the trophy room where dustsheets cover wing-backed armchairs and a lion skin is stretched out in front of the fireplace. I've only been in here once before, a long, long time ago. The door is usually closed, but now the room draws me in somehow. I take a step inside. Golden dust motes hang, suspended in shafts of sunlight. It smells musty, of cigar smoke and mothballs. Faded animal heads line the walls; zebra and antelope from a different era, a different time, when Sir William Knight, the Victorian trophy hunter ventured with his pith helmet and rifle into Africa. There are glass cases full of stuffed animals too. I recognize some from this country; an otter in a pose of eating a trout on a riverbank and a golden eagle on a rock with a mountain hare in its talons. There's an elephant's foot umbrella stand by the door. I touch the grey skin and it feels hard, like weathered leather. Somewhere in the house, a door slams. I freeze and listen. Distant footsteps clack on a tiled floor. I slide out of the room, glad my shoeless feet make no noise, but the damp footprints from my socks leave a trail that I hope will disappear before anyone comes this way.

I make my way to the east wing to Henry Knight's offices. The door to his secretary's office is open and Patricia sees me before I see her.

'Joe!' she says. She leaves the filing cabinet and comes over, her cloud of lavender perfume reaching me before she does. She opens her arms as if she's going to hug me, but I'm glad it's not an actual hug. It's more of an air-hug. I think she's worried the dog hairs and mud on my clothes will mess up her pale lilac suit.

'Joe,' she says again. She tips her head to the side. 'How *is* your mother coping? It must be so hard for her.'

'Fine,' I mumble. I hand her the envelope with the rent money. 'Mum says sorry it's late.'

Patricia puts it on the desk. 'Don't worry. She's had enough to think about.' She holds me by my arms and looks into my eyes. 'And how are *you*, Joe?'

I feel myself go red. Patricia loves nothing more than knowing all the gossip. I don't want to talk about Dad. Not with her at least. 'I'm OK,' I say. I try to squirm away from her, but I feel someone else's hands clamp around both my eyes and hear a girl's laugh behind me.

A laugh I think I recognize.

I resist the urge to kick hard back at her.

The girl laughs again and whispers in my ear, 'Guess who?'

CHAPTER 4

I pull the hands and away and spin around, but I'm not so sure I know the girl standing in front of me.

'Joe,' she says, a huge smile across her face. 'I've been wondering where you were.'

I just stare at her. Araminta Knight, Henry Knight's daughter. Last time I saw her it was September, just before she went off to boarding school. She's grown about a foot taller and she's wearing white jeans and a well cut jacket. Her hair is sleek and I'm sure it looks blonder. She's wearing make-up too.

'Hi,' I mumble. I take a step back from her. She doesn't look like the 'old' Minty I knew last year. Maybe being in year seven has changed her, like it changed the girls at school. At primary school they were a laugh, but something weird happened to some of them at secondary school. They started going round in gangs and you just can't talk to them any more. Maybe Minty's changed too. And she looks about sixteen, not twelve like me.

I push my hands into my pockets and stare at the floor and feel out of place in my old jeans and hoodie.

'What's up Joe?' she says.

I shrug my shoulders. 'Nothing.'

I feel Minty's eyes still on me.

Patricia clears her throat. 'Araminta, your mother wants you to be here when your brother arrives.'

'James is always late,' moans Minty.

'He'll be here within the hour.'

Minty slips her arm into mine and steers me out of the office. 'Come on Joe,' she says. 'Let's go.'

'Araminta!' demands Patricia. 'Where are you going now? Your mother will want to know.'

I try to pull my arm away, but Minty has my arm clasped tight and is steering me out of the office, away from Patricia.

'Nosy old cow,' she whispers.

Minty leads me along the corridor and back down the stairs into the kitchens. There's no one around, so she grabs two apples from a fruit bowl and throws me one. 'James is bringing his new boss for the weekend. He's just got a job in the city and he's bought a new sports car to celebrate. One of those open-topped ones. Apparently I have to be there to see him sweep into the drive. Mummy says I have to be on my best behaviour.' She rolls her eyes. 'She still treats me like I'm six or something.'

'Is Rupert home?' I ask.

Minty sighs and sits down on a stool. 'Haven't you heard? Roo isn't coming this summer. He's sharing a flat in London. He's just told us he's got a boyfriend and Daddy's not happy about the whole thing. Daddy refuses to speak to him.'

'Oh,' I say.

'Exactly,' says Minty. 'Daddy's acting as if Roo's died or something. Mummy's fine about it, but pretends she isn't when she's with Daddy. Parents! They live in the dark ages. We're better off without them.'

I stare down at my hands.

'Oh God, Joe! I'm such an idiot. Here I am going on about stuff. I didn't think. I'm so sorry about your dad.'

'It's OK,' I mumble. And it is OK. I'm fed up with people creeping around me not sure of what to say.

'I'm sorry I couldn't come to the funeral,' she says.

I shrug my shoulders. 'I didn't go either.' I look up at her. 'I couldn't face it.'

Minty says nothing for a while, but just munches her apple, watching me. 'Everything's changed hasn't it, Joe,' she says. 'I've wanted to come home for so long, but it feels different now. Smaller.' She smiles a half-smile. 'I even tried getting my model ponies out, but I couldn't play with them like I did before. It's like I've forgotten how.'

I nod but stay silent.

Minty tosses her apple core into a compost bucket. 'I want everything to stay the same here at Hartstone. I want you and me to be the same. I don't want anything to ever change. Ever.'

'Then you have to stay the same,' I say.

Minty frowns. 'I have.'

I shake my head. 'You've changed too.'

Minty glares at me. 'Have not.'

'Have,' I say.

'How?'

'Lots of ways,' I say.

Minty puts her hands on her hips. 'Name one.'

I take a step away from her. 'Well, for a start, you've actually brushed your hair.'

'Joe!' She reaches across and punches me on the shoulder. 'At least you haven't changed. You're still as rude as ever.'

I laugh and can see the real Minty is still beneath the designer clothes and make-up.

'Come, on,' she says, grabbing my arm. 'Let's get out of here. I'm taking you to meet someone.'

'Who?'

'Satan,' she says with a laugh. 'You're going to *love* him.'

CHAPTER 5

I follow Minty out into the stable yard and Weasel whizzes around us in excitement.

Minty bends down and Weasel rolls on her back to have her tummy tickled, squirming in delight. 'You have the maddest dog. Has she learned to retrieve anything yet?'

'Only food out of the bin,' I say.

Minty laughs and walks across to one of the stables. 'Over here,' she says. 'Meet Satan.'

I stare in over the stable door. A huge black horse has its huge bum facing us, and its head in the corner of the stable. When it sees us it flattens its ears.

'Meet Knight in Black Satin,' says Minty grandly. 'My friends call him Satan. He's evil tempered but he's a showjumping star.'

Satan continues munching his hay, watching us with wary eyes. 'What's school like?' I ask.

Minty shrugs her shoulders. 'It's OK. School is school. How about you?'

'Fine,' I say. And that's all there is to say. Minty's and my life don't cross anywhere but here.

Minty drums her fingers on the stable door. 'Come on. Let's ride out on the moor, like old times. I'll take Satan and you can take Bracken. She'd love to go out.'

'I'm meeting friends in the park soon.'

Minty puts her hands on her hips and pouts. 'You've seen them all year. I haven't seen you since September. I missed you at Christmas and I was skiing with Aunty Flo at Easter.'

'I'd better go,' I say. 'Anyway, you're meant to wait for James.'

Minty rolls her eyes. 'We won't be long. Come on, Joe. Pleeease! I've been so bored I might actually die.'

I shrug my shoulders. 'OK then, but we can't be long.'

She flashes me one of her big grins. 'You're a star, Joe. You tack up Bracken and I'll get Satan ready.'

I sigh and head to the tack room. I check the time on my phone, and see I'll be late to the park anyway. Minty has a way of getting what she wants. Besides, I wouldn't admit it to her, but I've missed her. It's a long time since we galloped across the moor together. She's a laugh. She does what she wants and says what she thinks. There's no one else quite like her.

I grab a riding hat from the tack room, and Bracken's saddle and bridle. Bracken and Bramble are two old Dartmoor ponies that are used as pack ponies to take picnics up to the shooting guests in the more remote parts of the moor where the four-wheel drives can't reach. Minty and I used to ride them out all over the moor. Bracken nuzzles in my pockets as I do up the girth. I can hear a lot of banging and cross words from Satan's stable and then see Minty lead him out into the yard. He trots on the spot, his head held high and nostrils blowing. He looks twice as tall as Bracken.

Minty climbs the mounting block, throws her leg over Satan's saddle, and slides her feet into the stirrups. 'Ready?' she says, turning Satan in tight circles to stop him cantering off.

I scramble on Bracken. 'Are you going like that?'

Minty looks down at her spotless white jeans and designer jacket. 'Mummy will stop me going if I go back inside to change.'

'Minty,' I call. But she's already left the yard in a clatter of hooves.

Bracken trots out after her and soon we are both on the track leading up the hill. The wet ferns brush against my lower legs and my jeans are soon soaked up to my knees. Minty's made it to the top of the rise ahead of me but I see Satan spinning and taking his front feet off the ground. Minty kicks him on, but he rears and spins again.

'Let Bracken take the lead,' I say trotting past her, trying to avoid Satan's hooves.

Bracken sets off at a fast trot and I can hear Satan settle down behind her. I turn in the saddle. 'Has Satan even been out on a moor?'

'He's from a top showjumping yard,' says Minty. 'He's used to fields and sand schools.'

'No wonder he's on his toes,' I say.

We ride over the hill and down into the next valley out of view of Hartstone Hall. At least Penelope Knight won't see her daughter riding out in her best clothes. I have to take the lead and ride in front of Satan past bright yellow diggers parked beside a row of newly converted cottages. Satan takes a wide berth around the diggers, eyes wide and nostrils flaring.

Minty kicks him on. 'He spooks at everything.'

I try to look inside the cottage windows. 'Who's going to live there?'

'They're the old pig sheds. They've been done up for the shooting guests to stay in. Daddy says the guests prefer to stay on the moor. It'll bring in more money too. He's got a top London chef coming for the season to cook for them.'

We leave the cottages behind and ride up the narrow

path of the steep-sided valley, beneath the twisted oaks. Minty has to duck not to be knocked off by low branches and we climb out on to the expanse of open moor.

'Race you,' shouts Minty.

I follow behind, Bracken's little legs pistoning beneath me. Clods of earth fly up from Satan's hooves and the heather blurs as we race across the moor. We slow down at the top of the hill, both Satan and Bracken snorting and blowing, and we walk side by side, the wind lifting their manes and tails.

Minty's beaming. 'I've missed this *so* much. I'm here all summer. We can do this every day. You and me. You'll have to come, Joe. You know Mummy won't allow me up here on my own.'

Penelope Knight taught me to ride so that Minty could have company on the moor and we've been riding out on our own since we were kids. We've camped out and been for midnight rides. We've spent hours up here together. It's odd really. I reckon Minty knows me better than anyone.

'Let's go to Devil's Leap,' I say. 'I haven't been there for ages.'

Minty nods and I'm glad because I don't want to bump into Jolly and Ryan and I know they'll be far from here.

We keep at a steady walk, letting Satan and Bracken stretch out their necks on long reins. Lines of white frothy sweat run down Bracken's shoulders and flanks and I know she must be glad of the breeze. I take my feet out of the stirrups and stretch my legs. This has to be the best way to see the moor. There's no one for miles and miles and the only sounds are the wind over the heather and a buzzard's mewing cry. The whistling notes of a golden plover rise up from the moor. I spy a glimpse of the bird running through the heather and dry grasses, before it crouches low again, the mottled black and gold feathers of its back perfectly camouflaged in the broken patterns of shadow and light.

The buzzard's cry calls out again and I see it above the far side of the hill, riding the spirals of rising air on its broad, outstretched wings.

Minty shades her eyes with her hands to watch it too. 'Jolly Jackson reckons there's another hen harrier about.'

'Really?' I say. I think of the male hen harrier Ryan wanted to shoot. 'Has he seen one?'

Minty shakes her head. 'I don't think so, but he said the Birders have been up on the moors again looking around.'

'Whereabouts?'

Minty points eastwards. 'Up near Kingsmoor,' she says. 'The land beyond ours is owned by the forestry and Jolly's seen the Birders up there too.'

I dig my heel sharply in Bracken's sides to push her on. 'Well, it's Jolly's problem now.'

Minty trots alongside me again.

'I'm sorry about what happened with your dad.'

I nod, but don't say anything. I don't know if she saw the video of him shooting the hen harrier. It went viral so I'm sure she has. I can picture it now, the pale grey male sky-dancing, soaring and tumbling through the air trying to impress the brown female flying low across the heather. Then, the sound of a shot, and the female spinning to the ground and Dad climbing out of his hiding place to pick it up, his face clear for all to see.

Minty doesn't speak for some time, but I can almost feel the questions building up inside of her.

'Joe,' she says. 'What I don't understand is, why *did* your father shoot a hen harrier? He must've known it's against the law.'

I slow Bracken down to a walk and turn to look at her. For someone who's grown up on a grouse moor, she asks some dumb questions. 'Hen harriers kill grouse, Minty, you know that. They kill loads of them. Loads and loads. They can eat so many that there aren't enough grouse to run a grouse moor. There was a study in Scotland that proved it. Your father can't afford to have hen harriers around. Hen harriers and grouse moors don't mix. Simple as that.'

Minty frowns and looks like she's about to ask another question, but a startled grouse spooks Satan and whatever

36

question she was about to ask is lost as she tries to stop him bolting.

I take the lead down the steep ravine past Devil's Leap. The waterfall is in full flow, and Satan snorts and sidesteps all the way, his head high and his eyes wide, staring at the rushing water. The sound fills the narrow gulley with thunder, and fine spray mists the air. Minty has her work cut out work to keep Satan from charging forward, while his hooves slither and slip on the wet path.

'It's flatter down here,' I call out. 'We'll have to wade through the river to the other side.' I push Bracken through the water. It's almost chest deep on her and I have to tuck my knees up to stop my legs from getting wet. She high-steps through the fast current, her sturdy legs footsure on the rocky riverbed.

'Joe!' Minty's voice behind me is a half shout, half scream.

I turn to see Satan rearing and spinning at the water not wanting to walk through.

'Hasn't he seen water before?' I shout.

'Obviously not,' yells Minty.

Satan spins around again and Minty fights to turn him back.

'I thought you could ride!' I say.

'Not funny, Joe,' she snaps.

I see a hint of panic in her eyes.

'I'll come back and you follow close behind Bracken. I'm sure Satan will cross with her.'

Minty nods. Her face is white and I see her hands gripping the reins, and holding on to his mane.

Bracken plods back through and I turn her again and start walking through the deep water. 'Keep close,' I call back to Minty. 'Follow me.'

Satan trots in behind but when he reaches the middle, he stops and pins his ears right back. His legs are fighting the fast water, and I can see his feet sliding on the riverbed. He doesn't want to go forward or back.

'Come on,' I shout.

'What d'you think I'm trying to do?' yells Minty.

Satan picks up on Minty's panic. He rears and spins, throwing Minty into the fast current. The water swallows her up and she tumbles over and over until she manages to dig her hands into the muddy bank. I'm about to jump off and help, but she emerges, a shapeless mud-monster, her face plastered and her white jacket and jeans now deep shades of brown.

She wipes the mud from her face and scowls at me. 'Don't you dare laugh!'

But I just can't help it. I try to cover my face and turn away, but it's no use.

'Shut up, Joe!'

But the angrier Minty gets the more I laugh until

my stomach aches so much, that I have to hold on to the saddle.

Minty puts her hands on her hips and glares at me. 'Finished now?'

I grin and realize I haven't laughed like that for a long, long time.

'Look at me. Mummy will kill me,' says Minty, trying to wipe the mud from her jeans.

I jump off Bracken and grab Satan who's made it across the river.

Minty takes his reins. She looks white and shaken. Cold too.

'I might lead him home,' she says. 'I can't face getting back on.'

'It's miles home,' I say. 'You take Bracken and I'll ride Satan.'

'Would you?' she says.

I let Minty give me a leg-up on to Satan. He trots on the spot, fighting me. I'm not much of a rider, but I've been around horses long enough to know they pick up on everything we feel. I try to breathe slowly and relax and let him settle.

Minty glances at me. 'It's not fair,' she says. 'I've had loads of lessons, and yet you ride him better than I do.'

'You and Satan are just like each other. No wonder it's a fight.'

Minty glares at me. 'What are you saying, I'm evil?'

I stroke Satan's neck. 'Nah! He just pulls ugly faces when he's bad-tempered too.'

'Shut up, Joe,' scowls Minty, pushing Bracken on at a trot.

I follow close behind. 'Though I'm sure he's soft and squishy on the inside,' I call after her.

'SHUT! UP!'

I just laugh and trot along behind her. I forgot just how much I love winding her up.

We ride side by side down the track back towards Hartstone Hall. 'I'll put Bracken and Satan away,' I say. 'You can get changed before your mother sees you.'

Minty and I trot through the arch into the yard, but it's too late. Penelope and Henry Knight are standing in the yard with James and a man who must be James's boss, a man in jeans and pressed pink-striped shirt.

Minty is dripping with water and plastered in mud.

Henry Knight does a double take then roars with laughter. 'Ericksson, may I present my beautiful daughter, Miss Araminta Cecily Rosina Knight of Hartstone Hall.'

Minty can do no wrong in her father's eyes. She's always been his princess, but Minty is watching her mother, whose mouth has formed a thin hard line.

Penelope Knight turns to me, her voice soft, but with a cold sharp edge. 'Joe dear, please be so kind as to put the ponies away. Araminta needs to change out of her wet clothes.'

I lead Bracken and Satan away and glance back at Minty. She's already arguing with her mother, who is frogmarching her inside, and I know that right now, I'd much rather be leading Satan than Minty.

CHAPTER 6

When I get home I'm surprised to see Mum up and about. It's four o'clock so I guess she's caught up on sleep. There's also a big white van parked outside on the track beside the cottage next to ours.

Weasel flops down under the table, exhausted from her day out.

'Oh hello,' says Mum. 'I thought you'd be back later. Did you have a good time with Luke and Billy?'

'I stayed at Hartstone instead,' I say. 'Minty's home.'

Mum raises her eyebrows. 'And how is Araminta Knight? Did you have to roll out the red carpet for her?'

'She's not like that,' I say. 'Minty's OK.' I grab a packet of biscuits on the table and start unwrapping them.

'Hey!' Mum snatches them from me. 'They're for the new neighbours. They've just arrived and I've invited them in for a cup of tea because their electrics aren't working.'

'I'll be in my room,' I say, heading out of the door.

'You'll stop and say hello,' says Mum.

I shove my hands deep in my pockets. 'Do I have to?'

'Yes,' says Mum. She leans sideways to look out of the window. 'They're coming up the path now. Mandy's going to teach at your old primary school and she's got a daughter who's joining you in year seven.'

I look for my escape route, but Mum points her finger for me to stay. She opens the door to let our new neighbours in.

'Come on in,' she says. 'I'll just put the kettle on.'

A short plump woman with frizzy dark hair walks through the door followed by a short plump girl wearing glasses and a sparkly unicorn T-shirt. She looks more like seven than eleven. Her mousy-brown hair is plaited in two long pigtails.

'This is Joe,' says Mum introducing me.

'I'm Mandy,' says the woman, 'and this is my daughter, Ella.'

Weasel wriggles out from under the table to greet them and Ella kneels down stroking her fur.

'She's lovely,' says Ella. 'What's her name?'

'This is Weasel,' says Mum, when I don't answer. 'Joe's dog.'

Mandy smiles. 'Ella loves animals. Always has done.'

Ella turns to her mum. 'Can *we* get a dog, pleeease?'

43

Her mum rolls her eyes. 'You know we can't. It's not fair on the dog if I work all day.'

I look between them. It sounds like a conversation they've had a thousand times.

Mum pours boiling water into the pot. 'Joe, why don't you go outside with Ella and throw a ball for Weasel while I make some sandwiches.'

'Weasel's tired,' I protest. But Weasel is up, her tail wagging looking for a game.

I follow Ella and Weasel outside into the garden, scuffing my feet and kicking the gravel on the path.

Ella hitches her jeans up her waist. 'You're so lucky to have your own dog,' she says. 'We can't get a dog, but Mum says I can have rabbits.'

I watch her throw the ball for Weasel.

'Do you like rabbits?' she asks.

I think of the rabbits hung up in the larder, the ones that Ryan's ferrets caught for the pot. 'They're OK,' I say.

'When I get them, you can come round and see them,' says Ella. 'I'm going to get two. I can't decide whether to get giant lops or Dutch dwarves. I've seen people take rabbits for walks on leads.'

As Ella rabbits on, I make a mental note to make sure Ryan mends the ferret cage where they escaped. We don't want to make enemies of our neighbours as soon as they get here.

'Is it just you and your mum here?' she asks.

I shake my head. 'There's Ryan too. He's my brother.' It feels odd not mentioning Dad. I don't want to talk about him so turn away to look out on the moor.

'It's just me and Mum here,' says Ella. 'Mum and Dad divorced. He's still in Bristol with his new girlfriend and my baby half-sister, Amber. She's dead cute. Do you want to see?'

Ella takes her phone from her pocket and shows me a picture. It's a baby. It could be any baby. They all look the same to me.

'She's sweet isn't she?' Ella smiles.

'Yeah,' I say, hoping I've sounded convincing.

Ella nods. 'I miss her. Dad too. Mum said the clean air would be good for my asthma, but really she wanted to get as far away from Dad as possible.'

I just stare at her. I've never met anyone blurt out their life story so fast.

Ella shoves her phone back in her pocket and keeps talking. She hardly draws breath. 'It's miles from anywhere here, isn't it? It took us twenty minutes to come up the track from the main road; mind you the potholes slowed us down and you can't see any other houses can you? Once we find a place to rent in town we'll probably move there, but this was cheap that's why we ended up here, and Mum wants a garden because she hasn't had one before and she wants to grow vegetables because we couldn't in Bristol because we lived in a flat. It was near the hospital, our flat, and it was dead noisy, but you get used to it with blue lights flashing all the time. It'll be funny being somewhere so quiet and it must be dark at night here. Do you get used to the dark?'

I'm relieved when Mum calls us in for tea. I can't stand another moment listening to Ella. There's no off-switch on her.

I sit at the table and grab a couple of cheese sandwiches and a handful of crisps and listen to Mum and Mandy yak away. At least Ella can't talk through a mouthful of cake. It occurs to me that Mum's never had neighbours, except for Nan and Gramps when they lived next door, and I wonder if she's missed having company.

Ella wipes her face and turns to Mum. 'That was the best cake ever.'

Mum smiles. 'Your mum says she's meeting up with some of the teachers at the primary school tomorrow to get to know them. It's probably a bit boring for you, so you'd be welcome to stay with us for the day.'

I stare hard at Mum. We hardly know these people and I can't think of anything worse than listening to Ella for a whole day. I want a day to myself.

Mandy turns to Ella. 'Would you like that?'

Ella grins widely. 'Can I take Weasel for a walk?'

'Of course,' says Mum. 'Joe could take you up on the moor. You'd like that, wouldn't you, Joe?'

They all look at me now.

I stuff a biscuit in my mouth because I don't even trust myself to speak.

CHAPTER 7

It's not until after lunch that I take Ella out on the moor. It's been raining all day and it's only in the afternoon that the clouds lift and we can see the dark tops of the cragged peaks. In the distance, the sky is black and heavy and there's more rain on the way. I'd rather stay inside and watch TV.

'We don't have to go,' I say.

'I'd like to,' says Ella.

I look at her. She's wearing an old blue fleece and jeans, and trainers. I wonder if I should lend her a coat and find some boots to fit. But I don't say anything. With any luck she'll get cold and wet and want to come back early.

'Come on then,' I say. I let Weasel out of her kennel and she bounds around us, excited by a new person on our walk.

Ella's on my heels as she follows me over the stone stile at the bottom of the garden and out on to the moor.

'Are you allowed to come out here on your own?' she says. 'All on your own?'

I nod.

She stops to pick up a stick Weasel has dropped for her to throw. 'Doesn't your mum worry?'

'Dunno,' I say. 'I've never really thought about it.'

'I don't think I've been anywhere just by myself,' says Ella.

I turn to look at her. 'What, never?'

Ella shrugs her shoulders. 'Mum let me go to the corner shop, but that was it. Our flat was right next to a main road. We had to get a bus to get to the park, and anyway, when I was younger Mum used to worry about my asthma so she didn't want me out on my own.'

I push my hands deep in my pockets and keep walking. I can't imagine being cooped up in a flat with Ryan. I reckon we'd have killed each other by now.

'The moors go on and on, don't they?' says Ella. 'It all looks the same doesn't it, so how do you know which way to go up here?'

I pull my hood up to block out the wind and Ella's questions. Her chatter becomes less and less as the hill gets steeper, and soon she's puffing behind me and holding on to her sides. At least I've found a way to stop

49

her talking. I sit and wait at the top of the first hill for her. She stops to breathe through her inhaler.

'You OK?' I ask.

She nods and looks around at the moor. Her eyes pause on Black Rock. 'Is that the tallest one?'

'It is round here,' I say.

'Can we go there?'

I shake my head. 'It's further than you think.' The truth is I don't want to go back up where we scattered Dad's ashes. I'm not sure I want to go there ever again. I point at the sloping top of the nearest hill. 'That's the Sheep's Back. We'll go there. There's a good view across the moor from the top.'

I take Ella down through gullies rushing with brown peaty water from the moor and we follow the sheep tracks that contour around the hills. It's quiet here on this part of the moor. It's not as dramatic and picture-postcard pretty as the moors further west, where walkers and cyclists dot the hillsides in their bright jackets and fluorescent Lycra. Henry Knight doesn't encourage them either, and they'd be a danger on shoot days, getting in the way. We pass the southern edge of Dead Man's Wood, the dark green rectangle of Henry Knight's small conifer plantation. The pines stand tall and regimented, planted so close together that sunlight can't reach through the branches. Dead Man's Wood doesn't have the soft dappling light of broadleaf woodland in the valleys. Nothing grows on this forest floor. It always feels dead in there.

Ella peers through the trees and pulls her collar higher as we pass.

'It's not far now,' I say, as I stride out ahead of her. Weasel keeps trotting between us or racing off into the heather.

When I turn, I realize Ella hasn't followed me. She's staring at a crow sitting inside a large cage made of wood and chicken wire. I forgot the Larsen trap was here.

I wish I hadn't brought her this way now.

'There's a bird stuck in here,' she says.

'It's meant to be,' I say. 'It's a call bird.'

'A call bird?'

I nod and walk back to her. 'It attracts other crows and magpies in there.'

'Why trap them?'

'They eat the eggs of grouse and other birds,' I say. 'If we didn't control them, we wouldn't have so many other wild birds out here.'

Ella stops to peer into the trap. She curls her fingers around the metal mesh and frowns. 'What do you do with them once you've caught them?'

I face her from the other side of the cage, looking at her through the wire. Ella's a townie. She won't understand why we kill them. Dad had no time for townie sentiment.

'We send them on a holiday to the seaside with a bucket and spade, and a packet of bird seed,' I say.

Ella's face reddens at being teased.

I walk around to her side of the cage. 'Do you *really* want to know?'

Ella turns back to the crow, peering into its small black eyes. It ruffles its wings and pecks at a buzzing fly. 'No,' Ella says quietly. 'Maybe I don't.'

A veil of cloud trails over Black Rock. 'Come on,' I say, heading off, 'let's go up on to the Sheep's Back and then get home. There's rain coming.'

Sheep's Back is one of the most popular places for grouse shooting on the moor. The shooting butts are sunk into the ground, so you can hardly see them, and the rounded summit allows surprised grouse to be driven over the hill to the waiting Guns. The wide dirt track allows four-wheel drives to get right the way up to the shooting butts, which is good for the older and less fit shooting guests who can't walk so far.

'Look,' says Ella. She points further along the base of the Sheep's Back, where we see a quad bike and a rider on a jet-black horse at the bottom of the track. This is where Minty and her brother used to race each other on horseback, but I guess James has switched to a quad bike now. James is revving the engine and Minty is trying to hold Satan from bolting away.

'I'd love a pony,' says Ella. 'I had a few lessons before Mum and Dad divorced.'

We watch horse and quad bike start off up the hill. At first Satan spins and won't follow as the quad bike races away, bumping up the track towards the top of the Sheep's Back. There's no way Satan will overtake the quad bike, he's much too skittish. Minty must know it too, because she steers Satan on another course through the heather, straight up to the top of the hill rather than contouring around on the track. Satan sets off, his feet flying across the heather. He's fast and heading in a beeline up the hill.

'He's going to win,' I say.

But I've spoken too early. Satan takes a massive leap across a gulley, but loses his footing in the deep heather on the other side and I watch him fall. It seems to happen in slow motion, Minty and Satan crashing downwards and Satan rolling over, his legs turning in the air, over and over, his full weight crushing Minty. I feel sick inside. Minty's grandfather died when a horse rolled on top of him. Satan scrambles to his feet, and shakes his coat, the broken reins trailing on the ground.

But Minty doesn't move at all.

All we can see are her boots sticking out above the heather.

CHAPTER 8

I start leaping across hummocks of grass and heather towards Minty, hearing Ella puffing and crashing behind me. By the time we arrive, Minty has hauled herself out of a ditch.

'You OK?'

Minty rubs her back and winces. 'Think so,' she says. 'That ditch saved me, when Satan rolled on me.'

James helps Minty to her feet while I grab Satan's reins and lead him out of the heather onto the track. He hobbles out, not wanting to put weight on his right front leg. 'He's lame,' I call out. I run my hands down his leg but can't feel any obvious lumps or bumps.

Minty limps over. She scowls at James. 'That was a dumb idea of yours to race.'

James rolls his eyes. 'It was a dumb idea of yours to ride him through the heather.'

'You made him spook, revving the quad like that.'

'Then you should've let me win,' snaps James. 'It's your fault you've got a lame horse.'

Minty turns to Satan and then looks up at me. 'Is he bad?'

'We'd best get him back and get some ice on his legs,' I say.

Minty winces again, but I don't think it's the pain of the fall this time. 'Mummy's going to be so mad at me. I'll have to ring her to call the vet.' She takes her phone out of her pocket and tuts. 'No signal.'

'There never is here,' I say. 'Why don't you and James go back and call the vet, and I'll lead Satan.'

'Good idea, Joe,' says James. 'I don't think Minty's in a fit state to walk back.'

Minty glares at James. 'I'm fine. I'll walk back with Joe.'

James swings his leg over the quad bike and we watch him roar off down the track while we lead Satan slowly back.

'This is Ella,' I say to Minty. 'Our new neighbour.'

Ella gives a little wave and shuffles closer.

Minty grunts an acknowledgement and kicks a clump of heather.

'I love your horse,' says Ella. 'I used to have riding lessons, but I had to stop. There was a really sweet pony

55

called Strawberry I loved to ride. She was a strawberry roan. They're really pretty aren't they? I used to plait her tail.'

Minty looks across at me and rolls her eyes. I guess she's not in the mood to hear someone new gabbling away about ponies.

As we descend towards Hartstone Hall, Satan's leg seems to be getting worse. I can see his lower leg starting to swell. He's walking slower, but I don't want to stop or we might not get him home.

Ella's eyes widen as she sees Hartstone Hall. 'Is this your place? It's like one of those film sets. Do you really live here?'

Minty ignores Ella and changes sides to walk beside me. 'I was so stupid to race him through the heather.'

'Go ahead of us and get some ice,' I say.

By the time Ella and I have brought Satan back to his stable, Minty arrives with an ice boot for Satan's leg.

'I'll hose his leg down first,' says Minty.

I try to hold Satan still, but he puts his ears back and hops about, rearing and striking out with his hoof. Minty curses and whacks his chest. 'Stop it,' she growls. But Satan won't let her near.

Jolly Jackson sticks his head over the stable door. 'Hello you lot. Having a spot of bother?

Minty nods. 'He won't stand still and I need to hose his leg to get the swelling down.'

Jolly rubs his chin. 'I'll get the twitch. We don't want anyone getting hurt, and the vet won't be here for another hour.' He disappears into the tack room and returns with a short pole with a loop of rope at one end. Satan flicks his head about as Jolly slips the loop of rope over the fleshy part of Satan's upper lip and begins to twist it round and round, the skin creasing up in tight folds.

Ella glances across at me, and winces. 'Is it hurting him?'

'It's a twitch,' snaps Minty. 'It'll calm him down.'

I look at Ella and try to make up for Minty's sharpness. 'Squeezing his lip makes him sleepy.'

'Endorphins,' says Jolly grandly. 'It releases endorphins in his brain that relax him and take away the pain. If you're a zebra and the last thing you see is a hyena hanging off your nose, you want a bit of pain relief. See?' he says, as Satan's head begins to droop and his eyelids sag. He hands me the end of the pole and turns to Ella, taking her in for the first time. 'Aha! A new face. Are you one of Joe's friends?'

'I've just moved in next to Joe.'

Jolly beams. 'You're the teacher's daughter in the gamekeeper's cottage?'

Ella nods.

'Hope it's all OK in there for you?' asks Jolly. 'I heard the electricity wasn't working.'

'It's fine now, thank you,' says Ella.

'Well I'm glad you're here,' says Jolly, rubbing his hands. 'We could do with a few more beaters to call on this year. You'd love it. I'm sure Joe's told you all about it.'

Ella glances at me and shrugs her shoulders.

'Well, now's your chance Joe,' says Jolly. 'See if you can persuade Ella here to help us out over the summer. I'll go and get a drink for all of you. Hot chocolate or a cold drink?'

'I don't mind,' says Ella.

'And some biscuits?' says Jolly.

Ella smiles. 'I don't mind. Whatever there is.'

Minty glares at Ella. 'Well choose something.'

'I really don't mind,' says Ella.

Minty turns to Jolly. 'We'll have three hot chocolates and those shortbreads that chef hides in the cupboard beside the Aga.'

Jolly laughs and heads to the house. 'Coming right up.'

Minty turns back to Satan and begins hosing down his leg with cold water. Her face is set in a scowl, and I can tell she's furious with herself for riding him out on the moor.

Ella pushes her hands in her pockets. 'What's beating, Joe?'

'Beating?' I say. 'You should come. When the grouse

shooting starts, Jolly needs beaters to walk through the heather to push the grouse towards the Guns.'

'The Guns?' says Ella.

I nod. 'They're the shooting guests waiting in the shooting butts.'

'And they shoot the birds?' says Ella.

I nod. 'Well, that's the point.'

Ella frowns. 'Aren't they protected by law or something?'

I can see Minty's scowl getting darker.

'They're game birds,' I say. 'People pay to come and shoot them.'

'But aren't they endangered?' asks Ella.

I shake my head and try to make up for Minty's unfriendliness. 'Gamekeepers look after the moors to make sure there are enough grouse to shoot each season. If there aren't we don't shoot them.'

Ella pulls a face. 'I don't know,' she says. 'I don't think I want to see birds being shot.'

Minty turns on her. 'Do you eat chicken?'

Ella nods.

'Well we eat grouse,' snaps Minty. 'And I bet the grouse I eat have a much better life out on the moor than your factory-farmed chicken pumped full of chemicals.'

Ella stares down at the ground, pushing loose straw with her foot. 'But . . . '

Ella's voice falters. I hope she's got the sense to keep quiet. I don't know anyone brave enough to take on Minty when she's in a bad mood, but Ella doesn't seem to know when to shut up.

'But what?' says Minty.

'Well,' says Ella, 'you kill crows too. I saw one in a trap. You don't eat *them*.'

Minty puts her hand on her hip and flicks her hair back. 'It's *because* we kill the crows and foxes that we have lots of other wild birds. We protect wildlife, but the problem is that bunny-huggers just don't get it.'

I can see Ella's eyes brim with tears. She steps back and leans against the wall, breathing several times into her inhaler.

'For God's sake,' snaps Minty. 'Are you a complete idiot? Satan might kick you back there.'

Ella's face is flushed. She's blinking hard trying to stop the tears. 'I'm going back,' she says.

I look outside. A fine rain is falling, gusted and swirled by the wind.

'Wait for me,' I say, 'I won't be long.'

'It's OK,' she says. 'I'll go on ahead.'

I hesitate. I can't just let go of Satan.

Minty turns her attention back to me. 'Hold him will you, Joe. I need to put his ice-boot on.'

Ella edges past and rushes out of the stable door. I hear

the splash of her trainers through the puddles receding out of the courtyard.

Minty rolls her eyes. 'What a drip.'

'Minty!' I say, 'She's OK. She's nice.'

'I can't stand nice people,' says Minty. 'They're boring. They never have opinions. She can't even decide if she wants hot chocolate or juice.'

I say nothing and rub Satan's nose. Minty's gone too far this time, but I don't dare tell her that.

'Talking of hot chocolate,' says Minty, 'here's Jolly with our drinks.'

It's not for another hour that I get to leave Hartstone Hall. I had to hold Satan while the vet examined him and then helped Minty bed down the stable with deep straw. She wanted to show me the blue eggs from her Araucana hens before I left too.

I jog most of the way back home through the mizzling rain, glad that I don't have to walk for Ella to keep up. Weasel keeps close by my side, trotting at my heels. The low cloud folds over us, veiling my sight and muting the sounds, so that it feels as if Weasel and I are the only things that exist in this grey nothingness. Beads of water cling to my hair and soak deep into the fabric of my jeans.

By the time I reach home, I'm cold and soaked to the

skin. It's early evening, but our cottage lights glow bright in the gathering gloom of a sky heavy and black with cloud. A gust of wind slams the door behind me, shutting out the rain. I kick my boots off, inhaling the smell of a casserole drifting from the kitchen.

'Joe is that you?'

'Yes Mum.'

'Where've you been?' she calls back. 'You've been ages.'

I enter the warm fug of the kitchen. Ryan is sitting at the table eating his supper and I'm surprised to see Mandy too. I wonder if Ella's told her mum about Minty not being nice to her. I bet she's told her mum I wasn't nice to her too.

'Hi Joe,' says Mandy. 'Did you have a nice walk?'

'Fine,' I mumble.

She's looking beyond me, to the door.

Mum is looking at me intently. Maybe I am in trouble. I feel guilty for not standing up for Ella when Minty was being mean.

'I'll get changed,' I say, heading back out of the door.

Mum's trying to look past me. 'Tell Ella her mum's in here.'

'Ella?' I say.

Mum frowns. 'Yes, Ella. Where is she?'

'She came back before me,' I say. 'She wanted to get home early.'

62

Mum glances back at Mandy. 'How long ago was that?'

'Ages,' I say. 'I can't remember exactly. An hour, two hours, maybe?'

Mandy takes a step forward, but she doesn't look cross, she looks scared. 'But Ella's not come home.'

Ryan looks up from his food.

They're all staring at me now.

'What d'you mean?' I say.

Mandy grips the back of a chair. 'We thought she was with you.'

I feel a sinking pit inside my stomach and look through the rain-smattered window, out into the cold and darkening sky.

Ryan drops his knife and fork on his plate and looks at me. 'You bloody idiot, Joe.'

And this time he's right.

I am an idiot.

I should have walked Ella home. She doesn't even have the right coat or boots because of me. Right now, Ella is out there on the moor, lost and alone.

And it's all my fault.

CHAPTER 9

Ryan gets up from his chair. 'Where did you last see her?'

'At Hartstone Hall,' I say.

'Which way did she go?'

'I didn't see,' I say. 'I was helping Minty.'

'Minty?' says Mum. Her eyes burn into me.

I look between them all. 'Yes, she fell off her horse and we helped her home. Ella decided to leave early.'

Mum narrows her eyes at me. 'Ella doesn't know the moor. You know that, Joe. You should've stayed with her.'

Mandy pulls her phone from her pocket. 'I'll try her mobile,' she says. She dials the number but her face falls. 'There's no connection.'

Ryan nods. 'The signal is poor in most places.' He grabs his coat from behind the door. 'What was she wearing?'

A blue fleece, jeans, and trainers,' I say. I glance out at the rain.

'Did she have her coat?' says Mandy.

I shake my head.

Ryan glares at me. 'Well done, Joe. Well done.'

Mum picks up the phone. 'I'll call Mountain Rescue.'

Ryan nods. 'I'll pack a rucksack with warm clothes, and head out and start looking too.'

'I'll come too,' I say, getting up.

'You've done enough damage,' snaps Ryan. 'You stay here.'

I sit down and push my seat back into the corner of the room. Ryan's right. It's almost July, but it's cold and wet out on the moors. Ella could be in real danger.

Mandy takes a sip of her tea, but I can see her hand is shaking. Her mug rattles as she puts it back on the table. 'Did she have her inhaler?'

I nod and think of how breathless Ella was walking up the hills.

'Horses make her asthma worse,' says Mandy. 'Did she tell you?'

I shake my head.

Mandy bites her thumbnail. 'I should have taken her with me today. I should have taken her.'

Mum puts the phone down. 'The mountain rescue team is going to Hartstone Hall, but they want to use a tracker dog. They're going to stop here for an item of Ella's clothing for her scent. Could you go to your house and find something?'

Mandy nods and heads home, looking relieved to have something to do.

When Mandy's out of the house, Mum folds her arms and turns on me. 'I might have guessed Minty had something to do with this.'

'What d'you mean?'

'What happened?' says Mum.

'Nothing,' I say.

Mum just continues to glare at me. I'm sure she can see into me or read my mind.

'So why did Ella want to leave early?' she says.

I look away from Mum, so she can't read my face. 'They're different,' I say. 'Minty's well . . . she's just Minty, and Ella is . . . ' I pause. 'I don't know. She tries too hard. She's a bit of a pain, I guess. She's too nice.'

Mum snorts. 'Since when was being nice a fault in someone?'

I stare at the table.

'Too nice?' Mum repeats. 'Are those Minty's words or yours?'

I shrug my shoulders.

Mum starts packing the dishwasher, slamming plates into the racks. 'Minty's as bad as her father. Henry

Knight has the same sense of entitlement. Thinks he owns everybody.'

I look up at Mum. I've never heard her speak out against the Knight family before. Then again, I've never heard her speak out strongly about anything before. Maybe she couldn't with Dad.

She flings forks into the cutlery rack. 'Ever thought why someone like Ella might be like she is?'

I don't say anything.

Mum rants on. 'A girl like her spends her life being nice, trying to please everyone; keeping her mum happy, her dad happy, her stepmum happy, her sister happy. She probably spends so much time trying to keep everyone else happy, that she's no time for herself.'

I open my mouth, but can't think of anything to say.

Mum wags a dirty ladle at me. 'Ever thought why they moved up here?'

'Because of her asthma,' I say. 'And because her mum wanted a new start. That's what Ella told me.'

Mum flings the ladle in the top rack. 'Partly,' she says. 'But Mandy also told me she moved because Ella was badly bullied at her old school. She was teased about her weight, about her asthma, about being geeky, about asking questions, and anything else they wanted to pick on. That's why Mandy left before the end of term. She wanted Ella to have a fresh start, with new friends and new people.'

I look down at my feet.

Mum slams the dishwasher door shut. 'And it doesn't even look like she can have that. Does it Joe?'

Mandy returns with a bag of Ella's clothes. 'These are the ones she was wearing yesterday. I hope they'll do.'

'They'll be fine,' says Mum. 'The tracker dogs are brilliant.'

Mandy twists the handle of the plastic bag around her finger.

'I'm sorry,' I say. It sounds feeble and useless, because it is. It's a useless thing to say.

'She's not used to being on her own,' says Mandy.

'They'll find her,' says Mum. 'It's cold, but at least it's summer. Hopefully she's found a place to get out of the rain.' She turns to me. 'Joe, get the fire going in the other room. She'll need to warm up when she's back and there isn't any heating next door yet.'

I'm glad to get out of the kitchen. I kneel in front of the wood burner and start building a stack of kindling followed by larger sticks and a small log. I light the firelighter, and watch the orange flames lick up around the dry wood and dance around each other. It's only now I realize just how cold my hands are. Weasel slides into the room and curls herself up on the rug by the fire and I stroke her soft head. 'I've been dumb,' I whisper. 'You think I'm dumb, don't you?'

Weasel licks my hand and wags the tip of her tail.

She doesn't mind Ella. All that matters to her is if someone's kind to her. Maybe we should be like dogs. Humans make things so complicated.

I switch on the TV but I'm not really watching. The rain is heavy now and constant, and the sky has darkened so much that it feels like night. I hear a car arrive and look out but it's the mountain rescue team collecting Ella's clothes for a scent trail. They'll all know up at Hartstone Hall that a girl's gone missing. I wonder if Minty knows now too.

I put another log into the wood burner and sit on the sofa, wrapping a blanket around me. Dad stares out from a photo on the mantelpiece. I know what he's thinking. *Stupid boy. Useless. Good job Ryan is there to save the day. Ryan the hero. Ryan who does everything right. Why can't you be more like Ryan?*

As if on cue, I hear Mum shouting from the kitchen. 'Mandy! Mandy! Ryan's coming up the path and he's got Ella. Oh thank God. He's got Ella.'

I flick off the TV and sit staring at the fire. I should go into the kitchen but I don't want to. This was all my fault. I just want to disappear. I want the sofa to swallow me up. Mum and Mandy bundle Ella through into the room and sit her by the fire. Mandy removes Ella's wet fleece and Mum wraps a duvet around her. Ella is breathing into her inhaler, her chest sounding tight and wheezy.

'I'll get you a hot drink, Ella,' says Mum.

69

Ella looks small wrapped in the duvet and she's still wearing the wool hat and gloves that Ryan took with him when he went to find her. Her hands are shaking and water is oozing from her wet jeans on to the rug,

'Joe,' snaps Mum. 'Go and get some towels and thick socks from the airing cupboard.'

Before I can leave the room, Ryan opens the door and stands in the doorway, his body filling the frame. 'I've told Mountain Rescue we've found Ella and to call off the search.' He turns and glares at me. 'Reckon you've got some explaining to do, going out unprepared, putting lives at risk. Only an idiot would do that.'

Mum nods and looks at me. 'We'll talk about that later, but an apology to Ella would do for starters,' she says.

Ella looks up and takes her inhaler from her mouth.

'It's not Joe's fault,' she says.

Ryan frowns and glares at me. 'He should've walked you home. He knows that.'

'He was helping another girl with her horse at the time,' says Ella. 'He told me to wait for him. He told me to wait and I didn't.'

Mum glances between Ella and me. I can see her trying to figure out the truth between the words.

'It doesn't matter whose fault it is,' says Mandy taking her daughter's hand in hers. 'You're safe and no one's hurt, that the important thing.'

Ella pulls her hand away. 'It does matter,' she says. 'It's not Joe's fault. It's mine, all mine. I'm the idiot. Not Joe.'

I just stare down at the floor. Ella could've dobbed me right in it, but she didn't. She's taking the blame.

I owe her one.

It's a brave thing to do and I start to wonder if I've got her wrong, all along.

CHAPTER 10

It rained all night and it's still raining in the morning. Mum has put pans and buckets in the boot room, where the water is leaking through the flat roof. It sounds as if it's raining inside with the steady *ting, ting, ting* of water on metal.

I pour out a huge bowl of cornflakes and I'm glad to eat breakfast alone. Mum's in bed after a night shift and Ryan's already out on the moor. I don't want a lecture about yesterday. I stuff my breakfast down and let myself out of the house, stopping by to see Weasel, to give her a quick run in the garden before I head to school. The lights are on in Ella's house and smoke is rising up from their chimney. I don't want to see Ella or her mum either and I guess Ella won't be starting school today. Not after yesterday.

I shut Weasel back in her kennel and head down the

long track towards the lay-by at the main road, where the school bus will stop to pick me up. Rainwater is pouring off the moor, cascading into the deep tyre ruts and swirling in the potholes. When Ryan and I were younger we'd race paper boats and see how far they would get. The water has scoured out the loose gravel, deepening the track, and I wonder if Mum's car will make it down here later. I pull my hood right up and keep my head down to stay dry. It's only when I reach the main road, that I see Ella standing in the lay-by, half hidden beneath an umbrella.

'Hi,' I say. I wait for her constant chatter, but it doesn't come. 'You OK?'

'Fine thanks.' She hoists her bag higher on her shoulder and stares down the road.

'I didn't think you'd come to school today,' I say.

Ella shrugs her shoulders. 'I have to start sometime.'

We wait in silence, the rain pattering on her umbrella, and the water rushing through a storm drain beneath the road. I want to thank her for not dobbing me in yesterday, but the school bus looms around the corner, its headlights picking out the raindrops.

'Here's our bus,' I say. And I feel stupid and self-conscious, because it's obviously the bus. It's big and yellow and has *School Bus* written on the front and sides. We're the fourth stop on its route and so it's fairly empty.

I always take the back seat and Billy and Luke join me when they get on, but I'm not sure whether to offer Ella to sit with me. If I sat next to her near the front it would just look weird.

Ella shakes out her umbrella and climbs on the bus ahead of me. She sits down near the front and places her bag on the seat next to her, so that I couldn't sit with her if I wanted to. I feel I should say something but she's staring out of the window and so I walk past to the seats at the back.

The heaters beneath the seats are huffing out hot diesel-fumed air that burns the back of my legs and fogs the windows. I wipe the condensation with my sleeve and watch the raindrops chase each other in wriggly lines as the bus picks up speed. The moor is covered in low cloud, and the heather blurs and dissolves into the monochrome mist. I lean back against the seat, and listen to the swoosh of the wheels on the wet road and the clunking beat of the windscreen wipers.

The bus descends the valley road, stopping in the car park of the Bird in Hand. The pub door opens and Billy makes a dash for the bus, to keep dry. He climbs in, shaking rain from his hair and makes his way down towards me.

'Who's that?' he says, nodding his head in the direction of Ella.

'New girl in our year,' I say. 'She's moved in the cottage next to us.'

Billy pulls a face. 'What's she like?'

I shrug my shoulders. 'Dunno.'

'Hey, did you hear Mountain Rescue were called to Hartstone Hall yesterday,' he says, his eyes opening wide at remembered news. 'D'you know anything about it?'

I shake my head. 'No mate,' I say. 'Do you?'

'Nah!' says Billy. 'Anyway, what happened to you on Saturday? Me and Luke waited ages and you never turned up.'

'I got stuck helping out at Hartstone.'

'You could've phoned.'

'Out of battery,' I lie. 'By the way, Jolly Jackson wants me to get some beaters for the new grouse season. Are you up for it? It's fifty quid a day.'

Billy whistles. 'Fifty quid? I'd love to but Dad won't let me.'

I frown. 'Won't let you?'

He glances out the back window of the bus as if his dad can somehow hear. 'Henry Knight's built posh new cottages for shooting guests on his land.'

'I've seen them,' I say. 'So?'

'So,' says Billy, 'Dad's going to lose a lot of business when the shooting guests stay at Hartstone and not at the pub. He's got no bookings from the grouse shooters this year yet. He's worried he might have to lose some staff.'

The bus jolts forward and I slump in my seat and watch Billy play a football game on his phone. I sit half watching, but I wonder if Mum will be able to keep her job at the Bird in Hand. Maybe Mum's worried and that's why she seems to have changed her views on Henry Knight and Hartstone Hall.

I'm secretly glad that Ella isn't in my form group at school. I see her at lunchtime joining the lunch queue and sitting at a table with Sophie and Lily from our year.

'Come on,' says Luke, stealing my last roast potato with his fork. 'Footie in the playing field?'

I look out of the window, across the houses and buildings. The rain-drenched stone is dark and grey against the rising backdrop of the moor.

Billy grabs my bag. 'Come on, Joe, what are you waiting for?'

I follow them down the steps, past the new sports hall, to the playing fields that run down to the footpath by the river. Deep pools and puddles lie across the grass and the far end of the pitch is lost beneath several inches of water.

Just beyond the playing fields, the river churns brown and frothed with white. A year ago it burst its banks and swirled across the playing fields and right into the sports hall. The sports hall had to be closed for half the year, while the floor was re-laid.

Luke kicks the ball across the pitch, and it skitters and slides across one of the wide puddles.

Billy charges after it, yelling as the cold water splashes up against his legs. He pulls a face. 'Ah! I'm soaked now.'

Luke laughs. 'Tough, mate.'

Billy smirks at him. 'Well, now I'm wet, I might as well score a goal this end.' He starts dribbling the ball slowly down the pitch towards the flooded goal, sticking his hand up, his forefinger and thumb making the loser sign.

Luke and I look at each other and nod. There's no way we're going to let Billy get this goal.

Luke narrows his eyes. 'Let's get him.'

Together we charge after Billy, the water flying up behind us.

Billy starts running, but the ball is slithering across the surface of the water. Billy kicks and the ball spins towards the further post. Luke launches himself at Billy but Billy dodges him, and I charge with them, shoving shoulders and elbows to get to the ball. Billy dives for it, his body skimming the mud, the surface water spreading in a wake behind. His head reaches the ball before we do, and the ball spins between the white posts.

'Goal!' yells Billy.

I kick water at him, a wave of frothy mud that fills his mouth.

He scrambles to his feet and kicks water back at me. Luke joins in too, and we're kicking and yelling so much that we don't even hear Mr Thorne striding across the pitch.

'BOYS!'

We all stop and turn, our wet trousers clinging to our legs. Billy is plastered from head to foot.

Well?' he says.

Billy smirks. 'We fell over, sir.'

Mr Thorne says nothing.

'We were playing football,' says Luke.

'Obviously,' says Mr Thorne, 'and so you should know that football has been banned on the flooded pitch.'

Billy picks up the football. 'We forgot,' he says.

'Well, let me help you remember,' says Mr Thorne. 'As you're all wet already you can help me carry some sandbags to put at the front of the sports hall.'

'But sir . . . ' pleads Luke.

'No buts,' says Mr Thorne. 'Follow me.'

Mr Thorne doesn't look at me or talk to me. He's one of the Birders who want grouse shooting banned. It was his video of Dad shooting a hen harrier that lost Dad his job and sent him to prison. Dad hated him, and he hated

Dad. Ryan refused to be taught by him when he was here and I guess Mr Thorne has got it in for me too. If I didn't like football so much, I wouldn't want to be in the football club with him as coach.

Mr Thorne's been trying to ban grouse shooting for years. It was him who set up a hen harrier project at school and raised money to sponsor a satellite-tagged hen harrier. Five years ago, it was Sophie's sister who won the competition to name the hen harrier, and she won with the name Storm. Their parents run an eco-farm with rare breeds and wild flowers. Dad didn't have much time for them. He reckoned they were just hobby farmers, but ever since he was convicted of killing the hen harrier, they didn't have much time for us either. Sophie hasn't spoken to me since.

I spend the rest of lunchtime with Luke and Billy lugging sandbags to the sports hall in a wheelbarrow.

'Lay them out across the entrances,' Mr Thorne says. 'There's more rain forecast tonight. If the river bursts its banks this might save the hall from flooding again.'

Our arms are aching by the time we finish.

'What about the match this weekend?' asks Billy.

'Don't know,' says Mr Thorne. 'It might be cancelled.'

Billy pulls a face. 'Cancelled?'

'Can't be helped,' says Mr Thorne. 'We might have to cancel the whole pre-season tournament if the rain doesn't stop. If we keep getting flooded like this, we might as well train you for water polo instead.'

Adam Thorne glances at me as he says this, and I know what he's thinking. I know what he'd be saying if Dad were alive. He'd be telling me that the flooding we've had over the past few years is due to the management of the grouse moors, allowing water to rush off the hills. There are plenty in town that agree with him too. They blame the floods on Henry Knight. There are only a few miles between the moors and the town, but sometimes it feels as if the people who live in them are worlds apart.

On the way home I take my seat at the back of the bus, and when I jump off at my bus stop, Ella is already walking up the track ahead of me. She's puffing and clutching her sides, but I don't want to catch up with her or overtake. I don't want to have to talk to her.

I walk slowly behind her, squinting against the bright glare of sunlight on the wet track. She stops before we reach the cottages, catching her breath.

I keep my head down and walk past.

'I'm sorry about your dad,' she says.

I stop in my tracks.

'Some of the girls told me your dad died. I thought your mum and dad had split up, like mine.'

'What else did they tell you?'

'Not much,' she mumbles.

I turn and see her face redden. I bet Sophie and Lily told her about Dad being caught shooting a hen harrier. Dad's name was dragged through the mud before and after he died. Mum hid the hate mail pushed through our letter box, but I found it anyway. Prison destroyed Dad. Hardly anyone went to his funeral. Only Jolly Jackson and the groom from Hartstone turned up. Henry Knight said he was away, but we all knew he was home at the time.

It's old news to everyone now, but no one sees Ryan closing up like Dad, folding inside himself and leaving us out. No one sees Mum working all hours to keep us afloat, and me stuck in the middle.

I push my hands deep in my pockets and turn to walk away. 'Well, now you know.'

'Nothing's black and white,' Ella calls after me. 'Seeing Mum and Dad fight taught me that.'

I stop and look out over the moor. A shaft of sunlight cuts through the cloud, a spotlight racing across the hills and valley, lighting up neon green fields against a slate-grey sky.

'Look,' I say. 'I'm sorry about yesterday. Getting lost and all that. You took the blame. You didn't have to.'

Ella shrugs her shoulders. 'It was my fault. I should've waited. I was upset, that's all.'

'Minty's not so bad when you get to know her,' I say.

Ella shrugs her shoulders and stabs the end of her umbrella deep into the dirt.

'Good job Ryan found you when he did,' I say.

Ella looks up. 'He didn't,' she says. 'I found my own way back. He met me on the way home.'

'Really?' I say.

Ella nods. 'I was lost at first. I'd no clue where I was. Everywhere looked the same. I sat and waited and got really cold, then I figured out the only one getting me off that moor was me, so I thought if I headed downhill, I'd eventually get to a road or something.'

'It doesn't always work like that,' I say.

Ella smiles. 'Well it did this time. I came across the track home and found my own way back.' She turns to walk up the lane to the cottages. 'You know what?'

'What?' I say, following her.

'I kind of liked it. I kind of liked no one watching out for me or telling me what to do. Does that sound crazy to you?'

'It does if you die,' I say.

Ella laughs. 'Well, I didn't die.'

I pause at the gate to my cottage. 'Like I said ... thanks for not dobbing me in. I owe you for that.'

Ella gives me a sidelong glance. 'I might hold you to that,' she says. 'There is one thing.'

I shrug my shoulders. 'Name it.'

She smiles. 'What are you doing this Saturday?'

I frown. 'Depends,' I say. 'Nothing if the match is cancelled.'

'Good,' she says, walking ahead. 'If it is, then you can meet me on the stile to the moor at ten.'

CHAPTER 11

'Where's Clueless?'

'Who?' I say.

Minty sticks her head over the stable door and rolls her eyes. 'You know, the girl you were with the other day. The one who got lost on the moor?'

'Oh, Ella?' I say.

'What a numpty. How can you get lost between here and your cottage? There's a massive great track.'

'She went the wrong way out of the gate,' I say.

Minty slides out of Satan's stable with an empty feed bucket in her hand. 'What are you doing over here after school, anyway?'

'Jolly's asked me to help him on the moor.'

Minty pulls a face. 'I thought you'd come over for a ride with me.'

'Come with us,' I say. 'We could do with a hand.'

'What are you doing?'

'Moving sheep.'

Minty rolls her eyes. 'He got me helping him do that last week. It was dead boring and I can't see the point in it. I mean, why bother?'

'It's to mop up the ticks,' I say. 'He gives medicine to the sheep to kill the ticks, to stop the ticks spreading disease to the grouse. We had loads of cases of louping-ill in grouse a few years ago.'

Minty stifles a pretend yawn. 'Like I said, it was boring. But it didn't stop *me* picking up ticks,' she says. 'I found one behind my knee, waving its legs at me. It was so gross. D'you want to see?' She takes out her phone and shows me a photo of a huge blood-filled tick, its fat round body about the size of my fingernail, its mouthparts buried into her skin. 'Disgusting isn't it? They're like mini-vampires. They don't care if I'm a sheep, a fox, a hare, or a grouse, they just want my blood.'

'So you're not coming with us?'

Minty shakes her head. 'Another time, maybe.'

A Land Rover rumbles into the yard pulling a small trailer full of bleating sheep.

'Coming, Joe?' shouts Jolly winding down the window.

I climb into the Land Rover beside him and slam the door.

'How about Saturday for a ride?' Minty shouts.

I think of the promise I made to Ella about meeting her. 'I'm busy.'

Minty replies, but her words are lost in the loud revs of the engine and the rumble of wheels on the cobbles.

I cling on as Jolly steers up the track and out, on to the moor. In the wing mirror I watch Hartstone Hall becoming smaller and smaller, and then disappear as we dip down over the hill.

Jolly brings the Land Rover to a stop. 'This'll do,' he says.

I jump out and help Jolly with the trailer, pulling the ramp down and letting the sheep out. We watch them jostle and trot on to the moor, snatching at grass before trotting forward again.

Jolly pulls his cap lower to block out the glare of the early evening sun. 'If only we could get rid of all these blasted ticks. The problem is the foxes and hares spread them about too. We might need another hare cull this winter to keep numbers down.'

I remember a hare cull with Dad two winters ago. Several gamekeepers from neighbouring moors came along too, to shoot mountain hares. Their white winter coats were no camouflage against the snowless hillside. By the end of the day the trailer was full of dead hares piled up high. I never knew there were so many hares on the moor. It was then that I discovered Weasel was gun-shy. She disappeared for three whole days and came back covered in mud and starving hungry.

'Come on,' says Jolly. 'Let's move these sheep up the hill.'

I walk with Jolly across the rough ground, the bees buzzing into the air as we brush the heather. Skylarks lift up high above us, their small silhouettes fluttering against the bright clouds, filling the sky with their song of summer.

'Can't beat a day like this, can you Joe?' says Jolly. 'I can't imagine sitting at a desk all day.'

'I have to at school,' I say.

Jolly chuckles. 'I know. I hated it too. I couldn't wait to get out on the moors. There wasn't anything else I'd rather do.' He breathes in deeply and stops to survey the moor. 'D'you think you'll follow in your father's footsteps too?'

I shrug my shoulders. 'Ryan will want to work at Hartstone. There won't be enough room for both of us.'

Jolly slices the tip off a ragwort flower with his stick. 'Joe,' he says. 'I know Ryan is upset and angry. I understand that, but I wish he wouldn't hold a grudge against me. I'm just doing my job. I want to work with him, not against him.'

'I know,' I say.

Jolly pulls the ragwort plant clear from the ground

in his never-ending battle to get rid of the weed. 'You'll have a word with him, will you Joe?'

I nod, but say nothing. It's not as if I talk with Ryan about anything any more.

Jolly grins. 'Good lad.' He slaps my shoulder as if it's all sorted. 'Good lad.'

When Jolly and I arrive back at Hartstone, there's a small, battered, red car pulled up in the yard and a man with a camera snapping pictures of the stables.

Jolly climbs out of the Land Rover and slams the door. 'Can I help you?'

The man turns to face us, his camera held at his chest, poised to shoot. 'I wonder if I might have a word with Henry Knight? I'm from the *Evening Post*.'

'He's busy,' says Jolly.

The man's eyes rove over Hartstone Hall, taking in the crenellated rooftop and the moor beyond. 'I wonder if he'd like to comment on the Ban Grouse Shooting campaign in town. Not only are town residents angry about the killing of hen harriers, but they're calling for a ban on burning heather. They say the management of the moor has increased the flood risk for the town. These last few days have proved the point.'

'As I say,' says Jolly, bristling, 'Henry Knight is busy, and this is private property.'

The reporter's eyebrows rise up his forehead. 'So

he's not concerned that he might be responsible for the flooding in town?'

Jolly's eyes flit between the man and Hartstone Hall. He turns to me. 'Joe, go and see when Henry Knight is available to talk.'

I nod and head into the house. Patricia isn't in her office. It's way past six so she's probably gone home. I can't find Estelle either, so I cross the entrance hall to the west wing of the house and hear Henry Knight's voice from the drawing room. I stand in the doorway wondering whether I should enter.

Henry Knight is talking about the grouse moor next to Hartstone.

'It's been sold, or so I've heard,' he says.

I take a step into the room and see the family in there. Henry Knight is sitting in his armchair by a smouldering fire. James is pouring himself a drink from a decanter on the table. Minty is sitting next to her mother on the sofa, slumped low, her long legs outstretched on a footstool as she taps on her phone.

'Sold?' says James, adding ice to his glass of whisky.

Henry Knight nods. 'To an investment banker, apparently.'

James leans against the fireplace. 'If he's got sons maybe we could get rid of Minty and marry her off to one.'

'Shut up, James,' snaps Minty, her face a dark scowl.

'Mind you,' says James, 'with a face like that, we'd have to pay them to take you.'

Minty rolls her eyes and returns to tapping on her phone. 'If you hadn't noticed this is the twenty-first century.'

'More's the pity,' says James. 'Life must have been much more peaceful when women knew their place.' He catches my eyes and winks. 'Don't you think so Joe?'

I feel myself go bright red as each member of the family turns to look at me.

'Ignore him Joe,' says Minty. 'He's being a complete moron, as usual.'

Henry Knight opens the door wider. 'Joe,' he beams. 'What brings you here?'

'Jolly Jackson sent me, sir,' I say. 'There's a reporter in the yard.'

'A reporter?'

I nod. 'One from the *Evening Post*. There's a campaign in town to ban grouse shooting. He wanted to know if you have a comment.'

Henry Knight's face darkens. 'Tell the reporter that I have no comment.'

Penelope Knight leans forward and reaches for her husband's hand. 'Don't you think you should say something?'

Henry shakes his head. 'It only gives more fuel to the fire. This'll blow over. There are some in town who want to blame us for everything.'

I know that if Adam Thorne has anything to do with it, he's not going to let it go so easily. 'What shall I say?'

James swigs back his whisky. 'Tell the reporter to bog off and get a life.'

Minty has already lost interest. She's tapping on her phone and smiling, her mind distracted by a conversation far from this room.

Henry Knight leans back in his chair. 'Tell the reporter to contact my secretary and put any questions in writing.' He looks across at his wife. 'It's best not to get too involved.'

I turn and head back out to the yard with Henry Knight's answer.

The reporter is leaning on the bonnet of his car and I can see Jolly in his office keeping an eye on him.

'Henry Knight says to put your questions in writing to his secretary,' I say.

'Thought he might,' says the reporter. He looks me up and down, taking in my hand-me-down tweed jacket patched at the sleeves. 'You one of the gamekeepers' lads?'

I say nothing and glance in the direction of Jolly's office, hoping he'll come to my rescue.

The reporter is still staring at me. He narrows his eyes,

a flicker of recognition on his face. 'Sad business about the last gamekeeper here.'

I feel my mouth go dry. I don't want to talk about Dad.

He leans in closer. 'Can't be easy for you, or your mum.'

I take a step back from him.

'If she ever wants to talk,' he says, reaching into a coat pocket and pulling out a business card.

I just want to get away.

At last I see Jolly striding this way.

'Henry Knight says to put your questions to his secretary,' I repeat loudly so that Jolly can hear too.

The reporter raises an eyebrow. 'Hartstone's been in the news a lot lately, hasn't it?'

Jolly bristles and faces the reporter. 'On your way, then.'

We watch him climb into his car and drive away, bumping over the cobbles.

'You OK?' says Jolly.

I nod. But I don't feel OK inside. I feel like I've been turned inside out. I glance back at Hartstone Hall. It's all right for Minty and her family. They're screened from questions and accusations from people who want to ban grouse shooting. They don't have to meet these people on the street. Minty doesn't have to go to school with them, or be taught by them. They're protected by thick walls, and shielded from it by people like me. Nothing can touch them.

They're protected.

Safe.

And for the first time ever, it feels so unfair.

CHAPTER 12

The Saturday match is cancelled. The pitch flooded but the water didn't quite make it into the sports hall, so I find myself waiting for Ella on the stile to the moor. Weasel bounds up to her when she sees her.

Ella's wearing a bright-red ski jacket and has a rucksack on her back. 'What d'you think?' she says. 'Mum got it from a charity shop. And she bought me these.' She points at a pair of walking boots on her feet.

'You want to go back out on the moor?' I say.

'Yup,' says Ella, nodding her head vigorously. 'But I don't want to get lost this time, so I brought these . . .'

She reaches into her rucksack and pulls out a map and compass. The map is new, one of the ones walkers use, with plastic coating. 'Just in case it rains,' says Ella.

'Can you read a map?'

94

'Only a road map,' says Ella. 'I was hoping you could teach me.'

I nod. 'Well, it's kind of the same.' I glance at her mum who is pegging washing to the line. 'Will your mum let you out?'

Ella looks back at her. 'She didn't want to at first, but she said yes in the end, as long as I stick with you. And we've got to be home by three. I've got some cheese rolls and drink.'

'OK,' I say.

'What about you? Do you have to tell your mum you're going?'

'She's asleep. She'll be fine with it,' I say. 'Come on, let's start off at Hare's Leap. There'll be a good view from there. We can see everything on the map.'

We set off, Weasel running ahead of us. The sun is warming through my skin and it's hard to believe it has rained for a whole week solid. The ground is damp and springy beneath my feet, but the older heather feels dry to the touch. The sky is blue and cloudless. Maybe summer is actually here at last. Weasel rummages through the heather sending a family of grouse whirring away from us.

I stop while Ella takes off her coat and ties it around her waist. I notice she's not as out of puff as on the first day. Maybe walking up the lane from the school bus has helped her find her hill-legs.

We walk single file up a track cut deep into the peat by years of water running off the moor. It feels cool and damp between the high walls of peat.

Ella looks up at the dark peat reaching above her head. 'The soil is so deep here.'

'It's peat,' I say. 'It's rotted-down plants and stuff. This stuff at the bottom is thousands of years old.'

Ella looks at me. 'No way!'

I nod. 'Funny to think there were bears and wolves roaming about then too.'

Ella laughs. 'Yeah right.'

'There *were*,' I say. 'And there were forests here once too. A thousand years ago there was the Forest of the High Peak. We did it in school.'

Ella looks around as if she's trying to imagine what it would look like to have trees rising up around us. 'So where are they now?'

'Where are what?'

'The forests?'

I shrug my shoulders. I've never really thought more about it.

She leads the way out of the deep track and up on to the moor. The vast expanse of heather covers the hillsides as far as the eye can see. It's broken into a patchwork quilt of greens and soft browns and the first flush of purple where the heather has been burned to manage the moor. The only visible trees are in the broadleaved woodlands huddled in the steep valleys, the dark-green blocks of conifers of Dead Man's Wood, and the Forestry Land beyond Kingsmoor.

'Why burn the heather?' asks Ella. 'All that smoke in the air. It's not exactly green is it?'

'It's been done for years,' I say. 'The grouse eat young shoots of heather that come up after the burns, and they shelter in the older heather.'

'So you burn the heather just for the grouse?'

'Well, I guess so,' I say. 'If we didn't have grouse moors, there'd be no heather. There'd be nothing but sheep. They'd eat everything.'

Ella's quiet for a few minutes. I think I've actually succeeded in stopping her questions, but she hasn't finished.

'But what if you didn't put the sheep in, what then?'

I stop and face her. 'What are you on about, Ella?'

'Well,' she says. 'Last year we did a project at school about the rainforests in Costa Rica. Lots of rainforest had been cut down and burned and the land used to graze cattle. The local people realized they'd lost loads of animals and plants from the forest. They'd had droughts and also floods and landslides from the bare hills. So, they took away the cattle and let the forests grow back.'

'And?' I say.

97

'Well,' continues Ella, 'the forests grew back quicker than they thought. And all the birds and other animals started coming back. And the flooding stopped and the people had clean water, and there was a big study to show that the trees soaked up lots of carbon. We even had a Skype session with one of the scientists. It was so cool.'

I shake my head. 'What's that got to do with here?'

'Well, what if you stopped the burning and grazing and let the forests came back?'

'Don't be daft,' I say. 'This is moorland.'

'But you said there were forests here.'

I roll my eyes. 'You're doing my head in, Ella. That was years and years ago.'

'But . . . ' she says.

'Do you have to question everything?'

Ella frowns. 'Don't you?'

I laugh. 'Come on. Let's keep going.' I've never known someone with so many questions. It must be exhausting just being her.

We cross several paths until we reach the top of the hill, where Ella sits on a large flat rock and spreads the map out in front of us. I start showing her all the landmarks and how the contours translate into the hills and valleys.

She sits on her coat, running her fingers across the moorland on the map and checking the peaks and landmarks in the distance. It must be so different to Bristol and I wonder if I'd get just as lost in a city with no landmarks to navigate by. I show her how to use the compass, feeling rusty myself, as I haven't used one for years. I haven't needed to. I could walk these hills with my eyes shut.

'Cheese roll?' offers Ella.

She reaches into her bag and pulls out cheese and pickle rolls and offers me one. We sit in comfortable silence looking out over the moor.

Ella lies back on the rock and shuts her eyes. 'It's so quiet up here,' she says.

'Except for him,' I say, pointing to a small black-coloured bird with a white ring of feathers on its chest.

Ella opens one eye and looks. 'Is that a blackbird?'

'Ring ouzel,' I say.

We watch it on a rock not far from us, bobbing and uttering its call. It doesn't seem scared of us at all. It flitters from rock to rock, watching us. I always think of it as Dad's bird. Out of all the wildlife here on the moor, the ring ouzels were his favourites.

'He's come all the way from Africa,' I say, 'He's probably got a nest somewhere and he's telling us to shove off out of his patch.'

'How d'you know all this?' says Ella.

I strip a stem of grass, throwing the seed heads into the wind. 'Dad told me,' I say. 'He knew all the wildlife here.'

'All of it?'

I nod. I remember how he seemed to know where to find every curlew and lapwing nest, and every merlin and kestrel. He just knew.

Ella folds the map carefully, concertinaing it together. She runs the flat of her hand along the edges, smoothing the folds. She opens her mouth as if to say something, but seems to change her mind.

'Right,' I say, standing up and brushing breadcrumbs and grass seeds from my clothes. 'I bet you a fiver you can't find your way back from here.'

Ella grins. 'You're on. Come on Weasel, you can show me the way.'

I laugh. 'Don't follow her. She'll only lead you down rabbit holes.'

I walk behind Ella as we contour around the hill. Ella's OK. It's actually a relief to walk over the moor with someone who doesn't know Dad; someone who doesn't judge me on what Dad did. It's like I'm seeing the moors for the first time. Maybe it is possible to put what's happened behind us. For the first time since Dad's conviction, I feel as if there may be a way beyond this. Maybe it wasn't such a bad thing, Ella and her mum coming to live next door to us.

But then I see it. Ella does too. We couldn't miss it. A male hen harrier rises up from the heather right in front of us. I feel the rush of air from its huge wings as it flaps upward. Its pale owl-like face turns to me for a moment, its bright yellow eyes fix on mine. It's just a fleeting moment, a fraction of a second, but it feels as if the world's stopped turning. The hen harrier is so close that I can almost touch the black wingtips. Then it's gone, sliding away through the layers of air, with the unmistakable body of a young grouse in its talons.

Ella spins round, her eyes wide. 'Was that a hen harrier?'

I nod.

'Mr Thorne has photos of them all over his tutor room.' She frowns. 'He says . . . ' She glances at me, and stops talking. I can see the sudden realization of the connection between Dad and me and hen harriers and the unanswered questions racing through her mind.

I push my hands deep in my pockets and stare out across the moor, to the pale-grey bird flying low over the heather. What Dad did can never leave us, because the problem wasn't Dad. The problem is the hen harrier on the moor. And where there are hen harriers and people who want to shoot grouse for sport, it isn't going to go away.

I know deep inside that this isn't the end of our problems.

This is only the beginning.

CHAPTER 13

'Oi, Joe!' Ryan barges into my bedroom and flicks on the light. I screw up my eyes and pull the duvet over my head.

'Five minutes,' barks Ryan.

I wait until he's out of my room, swing my legs out of bed, and rub my eyes. My phone says 4.15 a.m. Outside the pale dawn is speckled with the last few stars of the night. A long cloud lies low on the horizon, fringed golden by the promised sun.

I yawn again and regret saying I'd help Ryan and Jolly Jackson count grouse on Kingsmoor on the far side of the estate. I get dressed and go downstairs to the kitchen where Ryan is making porridge.

'Mum's left a note,' he says.

I pick it up and read it. 'She's off work tonight. She said we could go to the cinema.'

Ryan pours the porridge into two bowls, scraping out the pan with the wooden spoon.

'What d'you want to see?' I say.

'I'm fine here,' he says.

'I think Mum wants us to go.'

Ryan doesn't look up. 'You go. I'm fine here.'

I sit down opposite him and trail golden syrup in circles on my bowl of porridge. 'Billy's brother asked if you're playing five-a-side football down the club.'

Ryan's hand pauses mid-air. 'Billy's brother is a bloody hypocrite.'

I say nothing.

Ryan points the spoon at me. 'Billy's brother joined the campaign to ban grouse shooting and burning the moors.'

I frown and blow on my porridge to cool it down. Ryan's turning his back on his friends and on us. It feels like he's turning into Dad and I can't stop him.

We sit there in silence, the clock ticking on the wall and our spoons scraping the bowls.

'I'm making a go-cart,' I say. 'It's a school project. A green energy thing. Want to help?'

Ryan finishes his porridge and puts his bowl in the dishwasher. 'It's busy on the moor at the moment.'

'Remember when we made that go-cart out of beer crates and trolley wheels?' I say. 'Mum got so mad didn't she? We nearly killed ourselves coming down Robin Hill.'

Ryan's either not listening or doesn't want to. He pulls his jacket on. 'Come on. We'll check the snares and traps before we meet Jolly.'

I grab my own jacket and pass Ryan in the boot room as he unlocks the gun cupboard. I go ahead of him and let the dogs out. Weasel tears up and down as if she hasn't seen me for a week. I throw a ball for her over the wall and she leaps across bringing it back, with her tail wagging so hard her whole back end is wiggling from side to side.

Ryan sees her and scowls. I know what he's thinking. He's said it enough times already. Weasel is useless as a gun dog. She won't retrieve the birds, but she'll fetch balls and Frisbees all day long.

It's hard keeping up with Ryan. His long stride eats up the moor and I have to jog in places to keep up. We take the route around the Sheep's Back, past patches of blanket bog. The tufted seed heads of cotton grass glow white in the morning sun and bob in the breeze. Ryan checks the tunnel traps that bridge a drainage ditch, and I see him pull out two dead stoats and a weasel, and shove them into his bag for the stink pit. We make our way back down to the northern edge of Dead Man's Wood, following the dew trails of foxes. The musty scent of fox hangs in the hollows of still air. I watch the dogs with their noses to the ground and wonder what other trails they can smell. Ryan ducks beneath the low branches of the trees and I follow, entering the otherworld darkness beneath the conifers. My eyes adjust to the green gloom and I see Ryan's silhouette disappearing deeper in. My feet slide on the dry needles as I scramble over tree roots to keep up with him. I hear the dull thud of the dead stoats and weasel landing in the stink pit, and wrinkle my nose at the smell. You don't have to see a stink pit to know it's there. The stench of rotting carcasses lures the foxes in, along trails set with snares.

Ryan turns and walks parallel to the edge of the trees, checking each fox snare. I'm glad there are no foxes caught in the snares today because I'd have to hold Weasel tight against my chest or she'd run away at the sound of Ryan's gun. I know I'd feel her whole body tremble when the shot was fired.

Weasel's a coward, and I'm a coward too. The stoats and weasels don't bother me so much any more, but there's something about the foxes. I hate seeing them caught in the snares. Some struggle when they see us. But others just stand and stare.

I remember one. It was the time Dad handed me his rifle. It was a female, a vixen, maybe with cubs that were waiting somewhere for her to return with food. She stood there, her red coat glowing in the morning light. She faced me. She looked right into me as if she knew exactly what was going to happen. I saw it in her eyes, a fierce acceptance of her fate. I held the rifle. I was the one about to take her world. Her freedom. Her life. I remember my hands shaking and Dad telling me to toughen up and take the shot.

Toughen up. Grow up. Man up.

I looked through the scope to see the slits of her pupils widen as she took me in, the trespasser in her wild.

But I couldn't shoot her that day. Not even for Dad. I remember Dad taking the rifle from me while I turned away. The crack of the shot ripped through me. I felt it in my bones and in the silence that followed. It tore time apart, to the *before* and *after*. The *before*, when the vixen had padded on soft paws through the dark woods, and the *after*, when she was gone; her ragged russet body discarded on the damp earth. And it didn't seem to matter how many times Dad told me that the only good fox was a dead one. After all that time, I can still see her now, in her *before*, watching *me* with her golden eyes.

The sun has already risen above the moor by the time we meet Jolly at the first shooting butt. He's sitting on top of the turf wall, a thermos flask wedged between the stones. Bessie, his Labrador, bounds up to us and I crouch down to stroke her soft ears.

'Coffee?' says Jolly.

Ryan shakes his head.

'I'm OK, thanks,' I say.

Jolly swigs back his cup and shakes the drops on the ground. 'We'll count the grouse on Kingsmoor, and I must say, I think it's looking good. On the way up here I'd guess we're up to 350 grouse per square kilometre. And Kingsmoor usually has more.

I look across the wide moor, along the row of shooting butts spreading out in an arc up the long rise of the hill. I remember being part of a line of beaters last year that drove the grouse to these butts and recorded the highest number of grouse shot in the history of Hartstone. Kingsmoor is wilder than Sheep's Back. No vehicles can get up here and all the drinks and lunches are brought up by Bracken and Bramble. This is the best shooting on the moor, and probably in northern England. Henry Knight charges more for those who want to shoot here. It's as wild as it can get.

I scan the landscape for other people. The furthest edge of Kingsmoor is bounded by Forestry Land, where a straggly line of barbed wire divides a conifer plantation from Henry Knight's moor. This is the edge of Henry Knight's estate. This is where Adam Thorne filmed Dad shooting the hen harrier. He'd hidden in the forest, camped out all night, watching and waiting. I wonder if there are any Birders watching us now. I try to look for the telltale flash of light reflected on binoculars or a camera, but can't see anything.

Jolly's watching me and knows what I'm thinking. 'I don't think we've got company. I've been up here for a couple of hours. Bessie here picks up human scent and she hasn't caught a whiff of anyone.'

Ryan shields his eyes with his hand and surveys the moor.

'Well,' says Jolly shoving his thermos in his bag and rubbing his hands. 'Let's go and count some grouse.'

Jolly points out the beat we will be working, to count and record as many grouse and their chicks, so he can then work out how many can be shot this season. Jolly and Ryan send their dogs ahead of them. Ryan's pointer, Teal, heads uphill into the wind, her nose sniffing for grouse. I slip a piece of baler twine around Weasel's collar as a lead. I don't want her chasing all the birds.

The early-morning dampness holds the scents better than the middle of the day. I love this part, working with the dogs. It always amazes me how their hunting instinct is so much part of them. I watch Teal move through the heather, her walk slow and careful. She stops, her body becoming rigid, her nose pointing forward and her tail straight out behind. She lifts her forepaw and points to a covey of grouse hidden in the shadows. Weasel is straining to be free, but I hold her close. Widgeon, Dad's old black Labrador is grey-muzzled now and a bit stiff, but he loves being out on the moor. We walk in a line, calling grouse numbers across to Jolly who records it all.

The morning is warming up, and heather seems to trap the heat. An adder slides off a bare rock at the approach of my footfall, the flick of black zigzag on its tail, disappearing into the undergrowth. It takes a good two hours to walk the beat and count the grouse, and when we're done Jolly indicates for us to sit in the shade of a large rock beside a moorland stream. I let Weasel run free and she joins the other dogs for a drink in the water. She lies down in the shallows, her long tongue hanging out, panting.

Jolly pours out another coffee for himself and hands around a packet of biscuits. Ryan shakes his head but I take a couple.

Jolly's beaming. 'Well it looks like another good year, maybe even better than last.'

Ryan flings a stone into a deep pool in the water. Its ripples spread outwards, catching the light, and Weasel dives in after it. Ryan frowns. 'It's a good grouse year because Dad was the best keeper this moor's had.'

Jolly glances at me and then at Ryan. 'Your Dad was a great keeper, Ryan. No one denies that. I learned a lot from him and I want to carry on his good work. Do I make that clear?'

Ryan doesn't answer. He's staring out over the stream and across to a thatch of purple moor grass at the edge of Forestry Land. I see Ryan raise his head, looking, watching something. He's like a dog on point. He's seen something. I follow his gaze but can't see anything in the grasses. Jolly's looking in the same direction too.

'What've you seen?' I ask.

Jolly sits up. 'Look in the clump of moor grass to the right of the rock.'

I look and look, and then I see her, a female hen harrier. Her mottled brown plumage hides her well against the dry grasses.

Jolly gets out his binoculars and puts them to his eyes. 'I wouldn't be surprised if she's got a nest there.'

He hands me the binoculars and I look through, focusing on the dry grass. The female hen harrier fills the view. Her owl-like face looks fierce; her bright yellow eyes seem to look directly at me. I'm sure she's seen us.

Jolly pulls my sleeve. 'Look Joe, there's its mate.'

I take the binoculars away just in time to see a male hen harrier arrive in a blur of smoke-grey, carrying something in his talons. The female stands up on her long yellow legs, her attention suddenly directed up towards him. He's bringing food into the nest. He drops it at her feet before she has chance to fly up and take it from him. And then the male is gone, away to hunt again.

Ryan is already marching through the heather towards her.

'Ryan,' hisses Jolly. 'Come back.'

But Ryan doesn't stop. I see the female rise up tall again, face him and spread her wings wide, defending her nest. Jolly scrambles to his feet and follows Ryan with me close behind.

'Ryan, stop,' calls Jolly. He grabs Ryan's arm and pulls him around. I stop and look through the binoculars to see three small hen harrier chicks in a nest of dry grasses, the fluff of their feathers more like grey rabbit fur. The female has a dead grouse chick gripped in her talons.

Ryan takes the binoculars from me and focuses on the nest. 'One less grouse chick,' he says darkly, handing the binoculars to Jolly.

Jolly looks through them and frowns. 'I'm surprised I haven't seen this nest already.'

'Maybe you haven't been up here enough,' says Ryan.

'Maybe,' says Jolly. 'It's not been easy being short-staffed.'

Ryan stares at him, with challenge in his eyes. 'What are you going to do?'

Jolly says nothing.

'If you leave it, it'll take a lot of grouse chicks,' warns Ryan. 'That one pair of harriers could ruin this moor.'

'I know,' snaps Jolly. He scratches his chin.

'These harriers are here to stay,' says Ryan.

Jolly turns to leave. 'Come on, we need to think about this.'

Ryan narrows his eyes. 'The grouse are good this year because Dad kept the predators down. It's your decision now.'

'You don't have to tell *me* that,' says Jolly, wiping his brow with his sleeve.

Ryan watches Jolly. 'Henry Knight said this moor is the best grouse moor in England. He'll want to know we're keeping it that way.'

Jolly's eyes are scanning the moor for hidden people. He uses the binoculars and tracks them back and forth across the dark line of trees.

'There's no one up here,' says Ryan.

I hear the taunt in his voice, goading Jolly.

Jolly shoves his binoculars back in their case. 'I'll come back later and deal with them when it's dark.'

'The Birders have got night-vision cameras,' says Ryan. 'Best do it now, when there's no one up here.'

'I'll do it my way,' snaps Jolly. 'Let's go.'

Jolly trudges back through the heather to pack his thermos flask away. He doesn't see Ryan pull his shotgun from its slip, load up, and hold it to his shoulder. I know this is Ryan's payback, but I'm too far away to stop him.

'Ryan, no!' I shout.

Ryan takes several steps towards the nest and the female utters her alarm call. Ryan's hands are still, his right eye narrowed and his mouth drawn into a thin line. I can tell he has the female lined up along the gun-barrels.

'Don't, Ryan!'

Ryan never misses a shot.

Never.

The sound of gunfire sends shockwaves through my chest and down my legs into the earth.

A single gunshot, dividing the *before* and *after* of this bird.

I look across to where the hen harrier had once been, but there is only empty space.

All I see is a puff of pale-brown feathers.

They swirl and catch the breeze, drifting slowly down the moor, like winter snow across the heather.

CHAPTER 14

'Go on, Teal,' orders Ryan, urging his dog to retrieve.
Teal sets out, bounding across the heather.

Ryan opens the gun-barrels, ejecting the spent
cartridge. It flies like a red blur through the air. He
methodically removes the remaining unused cartridge,
replacing it in his ammo box, turns and walks back to us,
grim satisfaction on his face.

Jolly is just staring at him, his face red and eyes
bulging. 'What d'you that for?'

Ryan's face is dark. 'I owed it to Dad.'

'D'you want to bring all the Birders running over
here? They might have seen us already.'

Ryan says nothing. He whistles a low whistle and Teal
comes back to us carrying the body of the female hen
harrier. Even I can see a long aerial sticking out of the
dog's mouth.'

'You idiot,' snaps Jolly. 'It's got a wire.'

Teal drops the bird and now we can all see the satellite tag on the bird's back.

'Oh great,' says Jolly, 'there's bound to be someone watching this nest.' He snatches up his bag. 'Let's get out of here.'

I look at the limp body of the bird. Even in death it looks strangely perfect, as if in sleep. Ryan kneels down and cuts the strings holding the tag in place. He places it on a rock and brings his shotgun butt down on it again and again until it's smashed into tiny pieces.

Jolly swears beneath his breath. 'Make sure it's bust. We don't want anyone tracing us.'

Ryan scoops the fragments of the tag into his pocket and shoves the body of the bird deep in his bag. I see his hands shaking as he tries to cover the barred tail feathers, forcing them out of view.

'Come on,' urges Jolly. 'Keep your collars up and heads down.'

I hurry after them through the heather, keeping low. It's only now that I realize Weasel isn't with us. She must've fled at the sound of the gun.

'Weasel,' I call. 'Weeeeeaaaseeeeel!'

'Shut up,' snaps Ryan. 'Keep going.'

We head away from Kingsmoor, keeping below the rise, walking alongside the stream in the narrow gulley.

We all keep our heads down, just in case a camera is watching somewhere. Jolly marches ahead, whacking his stick against the long grass. It's not until we're passing Dead Man's Wood that Jolly leads us under the trees, where we stand in the grim darkness looking out at the moor. He searches the slopes for signs of people watching.

'There's no one there,' says Ryan.

Jolly spins around and shoves the end of his stick in Ryan's chest. 'Never, ever do that again. Understand?'

Ryan glares at him. 'Someone had to do it.'

Jolly pushes Ryan backwards with his stick. 'I'm the head keeper now. Do you get that? Someone might have seen us. Maybe they already have. Our names might be being handed to the police right now. Is that what you want? To end up in prison like your dad?'

Ryan's hands clench and unclench. 'My dad was the best keeper this moor's ever had.'

'Your dad couldn't control his gun, or keep his mouth shut,' spits Jolly.

Ryan pushes the stick away and steps closer to Jolly so their faces are almost touching. 'My dad had guts which is more than you'll ever have.'

Jolly's face is red. Spittle fizzles at the corners of his mouth. 'I don't want you on this moor, Ryan. And I'll do whatever I can to get you out.'

Jolly spins around and heads towards Hartstone Hall, leaving us in the dark silence of the trees.

Ryan watches him go and spits on the ground where he stood. 'Bloody coward. I hate him.'

'I've got to go back up the moor,' I say.

Ryan turns to look at me.

'Weasel's gone,' I say. 'She disappeared after the shot.'

'We're not going back up there,' he snaps.

'But Ryan . . . '

'No, Joe. She'll have to find her own way back. If she can't she's not much use to anyone.'

I look up to the moor, hoping to see her tail bobbing above the heather. I whistle but Ryan glares at me.

'Shut up, Joe. Jolly's right. If there aren't Birders out there now, there will be soon. I'll get rid of this bird.'

I watch Ryan go deep into the forest until I lose him from view. I slide in after him, keeping myself hidden behind the trees and watch as he digs a shallow grave for it, covering it with pine needles. It'll be gone in a day or two. Some hungry fox won't pass by the chance of an easy meal.

'Come on, let's get home,' he grunts.

I follow him back, jogging to keep up with his pace. I keep my face down. I feel guilty. I am guilty. I watched a hen harrier being shot and I didn't stop it happening.

I didn't stop Ryan. It feels as if there are eyes watching us all over the moor. I daren't look up. But I want to know where Weasel is. Maybe a Birder has found her and they'll know she belongs to me. Maybe she'll lead them to the body of the hen harrier.

Ryan slows to give me chance to walk alongside him as we get near home. 'Not a word to Mum,' he says.

'I know,' I say.

'Or anyone,' says Ryan.

'I know,' I snap. As if I would. We had enough trouble after Dad got convicted.

We're almost home and I pick up my pace, but Ryan halts so suddenly that I bump into him. In the shadow of a single oak tree we see a figure, watching us.

I feel my heart hammer in my chest. So we've been seen. It's going to begin all over again, not with Dad this time, but with Ryan and me.

Ryan walks forward, his stride casual, but he keeps his dogs close and they walk stiff and alert.

The figure steps out into the light and when I see who it is, relief floods through me.

'Ella. What are you doing here?' My voice has accusation in it and I see her frown.

'I'm going for a walk on the moor. Mum's out, but she said I can go as far as the top of Hare's Leap on my own.

'OK,' I say. I glance behind us, half expecting to see someone following us.

Ella tips her head to the side. 'D'you want to come?'

'Another time,' I say.

'Can I take Weasel?'

'She's out catching rabbits somewhere,' I lie.

'Joe! Come on!' calls Ryan. He's already walking away towards the house.

I open my mouth but can't think of anything to say to Ella, so I turn and trot after him.

My mind can't stop turning over and over, worrying if we have been seen. Maybe police are studying video footage right now. Maybe the hen harrier's body has already been found. Ryan didn't take the identification rings off its leg, so they'll know which bird it was. I hurry after Ryan, slip into the house and bolt the door. Ryan empties his pocket into the bin, pushing the pieces of broken satellite tag to the bottom, covering it with rubbish. I stare out at the hill from the dark safety of our kitchen. It feels as if we're a pair of foxes that have gone to ground. But we can't stay in here for ever. Out there are the Birders who will want to catch us. They'll bide their time, lay their snares, and hunt us down.

CHAPTER 15

'Joe . . . is that you?'

Mum opens the kitchen door and walks in, wrapped in her dressing gown. She's coming off night shifts and usually I'm glad to see her, but right now I wish she wasn't here.

'You're back early,' she says, eyeing both of us. 'I didn't think you'd be back until this afternoon.'

'Came back to grab some lunch,' says Ryan.

The oven clock says it's not yet 11.00 a.m.

Mum looks between us. 'Is everything OK?'

'Fine,' Ryan and I answer in unison.

Mum frowns, trying to work out the lie. 'Well, we've nothing in the house to eat,' she says. 'I'll have to go to town.'

Ryan glances at his watch. 'I'll come and help.'

Mum stares at him. 'Really?'

'Yeah,' he says. 'I'll get changed first.'

Mum watches as he leaves the room. 'What's going on?'

I can't look her in the eye. Ryan never helps Mum with the shopping, but I guess that he wants to be far away from the moor so that he has proof he wasn't there.

'I thought we'd go out to the cinema tonight?' says Mum. 'The three of us.'

I nod. 'Cool.'

Mum's silent, watching me. She knows something's up. 'You coming shopping with us too?'

'I've got homework,' I say.

Mum's eyebrows shoot up. 'Homework? Really? You usually leave it till Monday morning.'

I do have homework, but I also need time to sort out the thoughts running through my head. I want to know where Weasel is too.

'Right,' says Mum, still staring at me. 'You'd better go and make a start on it. See you later then.'

I climb the stairs to my room and sit down at my desk. I have to redo my geography homework, as I didn't get a good mark in the last piece. Mr Thorne's writing is precise and neat. Red lines criss-cross my work. He doesn't miss a thing and I wonder if he was watching us this morning. I correct my homework, conscious of Mr Thorne's presence, and shut the workbook, shoving it deep into the darkness of my school bag.

I hear Mum's car cough into life and look out of the window to see her and Ryan bumping down the track. Mandy's car isn't in the drive either and I guess she's still out too. I look out at the moor, hoping to see Weasel. Maybe the sound of gunshot scared her so much she ran in blind panic and now she's lost. Maybe she's caught in one of the fox snares. My stomach turns at the thought of it. I imagine her struggling to get free, the wire tight on her leg or even her neck. I imagine her yelping for me to find her. It's hot on the moor now too, and if she's stuck she won't have food or water. I can't get the image from my mind. I run downstairs, grab a water bottle, and leave the house, locking the door and hiding the key in the ferret cage.

I can feel sweat trickling down the inside of my T-shirt before I've even reached the top of the hill. If I don't find Weasel in Dead Man's Wood, I'll have to return to Kingsmoor. If anyone sees me, they can't prove I've done anything wrong. Can they? As I reach the rise, I see Ella coming towards me with Weasel trotting at her feet.

'Weasel,' I yell. Weasel hears me, and bounds over, her tail between her legs as if she thinks she's done something wrong. I crouch down to give her ears a rub, but she races away from me back to Ella and jumps up around her.

'You found her,' I say.

Ella hurries towards me.

'Where was she?' I ask.

I'm so busy trying to check that Weasel doesn't have any injuries, that at first I don't see that Ella has something bundled in the jumper in her arms.

'Weasel found a bird,' says Ella. 'She brought it to me.'

'A bird?' I say. The first thing I think is that Weasel has found the body of the dead female hen harrier. If it is, it's the first bird she's ever retrieved in her entire life. But I feel sick inside. No one must know about the hen harrier. Ever. I feel my heart thump in my chest.

'What shall we do?' says Ella. 'I don't know where she found it.'

She pulls away a corner of her jumper and I see the bird wrapped inside. But it's not the female hen harrier. It's a gangly chick, with ash-grey fluff and it's very much alive. It stares at me from fierce dark eyes. I try to pull the jumper back further but it claws at me, and tries to peck my hand. It's only young but it's already fighting for its life.

'What is it?' whispers Ella.

I don't say anything, although I know exactly what it is. Weasel must have run back to the nest and picked it up. There is nothing else it can be.

It's one of the hen harrier chicks.

CHAPTER 16

'What is it?' Ella asks again.

'A bird,' I say.

'Duh! You don't say!' She rolls her eyes.

I just stare at the chick.

'I reckon it's a bird of prey,' Ella says. 'I mean look at that beak and those talons.'

'It is,' I say. I glance up at the hill, worried someone is watching us.

'What bird is it?' persists Ella.

'Come on,' I say. 'Let's get back.'

Weasel bounds around our heels excited by her discovery as I set a fast pace home.

Ella trots to keep up. 'Where are we going?'

She follows me over the stile and into the garden. Mum isn't back yet and Ella's house looks empty.

I pull Ella into the shadow of Dad's work shed. 'Wait here.'

I shove Weasel into her kennel and hurry into the house. Ryan's got Dad's key to his shed somewhere in his bedroom. I push open his door. His room is neat and tidy, clothes folded on the bed, the files for his gamekeepers' course stacked on his desk. The key could be anywhere. I pull out drawers and hunt beneath socks but can't find what I'm looking for. I crouch down and look under the bed, pulling out Ryan's old wooden toy box, the one he kept his Transformers in. I open up the box to his childhood. Inside are photos of Dad, an old whistle, a broken Transformer toy, and a cap pistol. Beneath them all is a single rusty key. I shove it in my pocket, slide the box under the bed, and run back outside to Ella.

Ella looks up from the small chick bundled in her arms. It's so tiny it fits within her cupped hands.

'I've got the key,' I say. I slide it in the lock and turn, hearing the bolt slide open. My mouth feels dry. I haven't been in here since Dad died. I hardly ever came in before. It was Dad's place, full of his gamekeeping bits and pieces. I half expect him to be waiting inside. I take a step through the door.

The shed smells musty. Weak light squints through the two small dust-encrusted windows. I want to switch on the light, but I don't want to risk anyone seeing us here. The shed is neat and tidy just as Dad left it. His workbench is clear. Labelled tins and jam jars containing screws and nails line the shelves. Secateurs and wire cutters are hanging against the wall. On the high shelves are bottles, some of brown glass with skulls and crossbones warning of their poison.

I reach beneath the shelves and start pulling out boxes. I have to lie on my side to reach what I am looking for. 'Found it,' I say.

I pull out a wire cage, one for transporting pheasant poults, and an old dustsheet from beneath the paints. I fold it in the base of the cage. 'Put the chick in here,' I say.

Ella crouches next to me and lowers the chick into the cage. It scrabbles away from us, pushing itself backwards on its pale yellow legs. It opens its sharp beak and glares at us.

I grip the edges of the cage. I don't know what to do. I'm not sure what I'd have done if I'd found the chick instead of Ella. Maybe I'd have left it out on the moor for the foxes to eat. I wouldn't have brought it home, that's for sure.

I can feel Ella watching me.

'It's a hen harrier, isn't it?' she says quietly.

I nod. My mind is turning over so fast, like wheels spinning on ice, and I can't grip on to any plan of action or ideas of what to do next.

'Mr Thorne will know what to do,' says Ella. 'He

volunteers for the bird charity and has lots of contacts there.'

'No,' I snap.

'But he'll know someone who can take care of it.'

I pull the cage away from her so hard the little chick falls on to its side. 'No one must know, Ella. No one. Ever.'

Ella fiddles with the end of her plait, her face pulled into a frown. Her voice is controlled, yet I hear the unspoken accusation in it. 'Adam Thorne might know where its nest is. He could put it back with its mother.'

I shake my head. I know she knows. I can tell she's guessed. 'We can't,' I say.

The silence hangs heavy in the air between us so thick that I can hardly breathe.

'Ryan killed it,' I say. 'The female hen harrier, I mean.' I rest my head against the cage because I feel suffocated. What has happened is happening again. 'If Mr Thorne finds out he'll be up here with the police. They'll know what Ryan's done. He could go to prison like Dad.'

'But it's illegal to kill a hen harrier,' says Ella.

'Well go on then,' I blurt out. I can feel hot tears in my eyes. I get up and look out the window so Ella can't see. 'Tell your Mr Thorne. Tell him Ryan shot a hen harrier, just so the town can hate us even more.' I wipe furiously at the tears.

'I'm no snitch,' says Ella. 'You know that.'

I turn to look at her. 'You won't tell?'

Ella shakes her head. 'But we can't let it die, Joe.'

I stare at the chick. It's sitting quietly now, watching us with its dark eyes. 'I don't know who can help,' I say. 'I don't know who to give it to.'

'Why don't *we* look after it,' says Ella.

'What, us? You and me?'

Ella nods.

'It's not that easy,' I say.

'We could try,' she says. 'It'll give it a chance. What will it eat?'

I frown and wrack my brains. 'Ryan knows a falconer who feeds day-old chicken chicks to his birds of prey. We could try feeding it them. We've got some in the freezer that Ryan gives to his ferrets.'

Ella wrinkles her nose. 'That's gross. Where do they come from?'

'They're from the chicken farms. They can't keep the male chicks, cos they don't lay eggs, so they kill them all on day one.'

'Ugh!' says Ella. 'That's horrible. I never knew.'

'I'll get one,' I say. 'I leave the shed and go back to the boot room where four of the day-old chicks are thawing on a plate. I take one and replace it with one from the freezer so Ryan won't notice.

I return to the shed and start chopping up the chick

with my penknife. Maybe the harrier chick has just caught a whiff of food, because it watches my every move. I hold up a piece and move it closer to the chick's beak.

'That's too big isn't it?' says Ella.

'It's what the mother would give,' I say.

The harrier chick backs away at first, but then reaches up, neck outstretched for the small lump of meat. It gulps it down and we can see the shape of a chick's head passing down its throat. It swallows several times, forcing it down and then opens its beak for more. I chop another piece to feed and Ella moves closer.

'Can I have a go?'

I pass a piece of meat to Ella and she feeds it to the harrier chick. 'How much does it need?'

I shrug my shoulders.

'I'll find out,' says Ella. 'I'll google it tonight.'

My phone buzzes with a text inside my pocket. 'It's Mum,' I say. 'She's on her way back. I cover the cage with another dustsheet and stand up. 'We have to go.'

Ella pulls the sheet around the base, covering the wire mesh, excluding any draughts. 'D'you think it'll be cold?'

I look at the little chick. It's huddled, belly full, but shivering. It needs its mother for warmth still.

I lie on my side and reach beneath the shelves again and pull out some of the kit Dad used to rear young pheasants. I lift up an infrared lamp and wipe the dust from it. 'I don't know if it still works.'

'Try it,' says Ella.

I plug it in and a warm red glow fills the room. I flick it off again. 'No one must see.'

Ella lifts the infrared light on top of the cage and slides them both under the workbench. She barricades it in with more dust sheets and some wooden panels. 'There,' she says, flicking the light on again. 'It's covered. No one will see.'

I check the time. 'Ella, we have to go.'

'We'll need to feed it tonight,' says Ella.

'Ryan can't know,' I say.

'I'll come,' says Ella. 'Text me when it safe, when Ryan's watching TV or something.'

'We're all going to the cinema tonight,' I say. 'Wait until you see our car leave and do it then.'

I lock the door after us, and show Ella where we'll hide the key inside a rhubarb pot.

It's not until I'm inside the house that it really hits me. I don't know what to do. I don't see how we can keep a hen harrier chick in the shed without Ryan finding out, and I don't know who to give it to without getting Ryan in trouble. It's impossible either way.

I help Mum and Ryan unpack the shopping when they return, and sit down with them for a bowl of soup and crusty bread.

Weasel snuffles for fallen crumbs on the floor.

Ryan looks up from his bowl. 'You found your dog then?'

'She came home by herself,' I say.

Ryan glares at me. 'A dog should work for its keep, like the rest of us.'

'She's OK,' I say. 'She's young. She'll learn.'

Ryan grunts. 'She's useless. She's never even brought back a bird.'

I stare down at the table. I don't say anything. I don't know what Ryan would do if he found out Weasel brought a hen harrier chick home and I don't know if I can keep it hidden. It feels as if I'm underwater, holding my breath, and I know at some point I'll have to break the surface again and breathe.

CHAPTER 17

Ella and I manage to meet or share the feeding of the hen harrier chick over the next few days, sending texts to arrange feeding times. I do most of the early-morning feeds and Ella does the late shifts, and we muddle through the other feed times, avoiding Mum, Mandy, and Ryan.

Each time it greets us with its piping call, eager for food. Each time it seems a little stronger and its head less wobbly. It can now sit on its haunches and balances with its legs tucked beneath it.

I can't stop thinking about it. It fills my thoughts and I can't concentrate in class.

I'm paranoid that Mr Thorne is watching me more closely. Does he know?

In maths class a screwed up piece of paper hits the side of my head.

132

'Oi,' whispers Billy. 'What's the matter?'

I turn to look at him. 'Huh?'

'I've been talking to you. Are you deaf or something?'

'Nah, just thinking.'

'D'you want to come to mine before football practice?' says Billy. 'Luke's coming too. Mum's making cheesy chips for us.'

'Cool,' I say.

'We're playing the Stingers on Friday. They've got a mean goalie, apparently. Good job we've got you as striker.'

'Yeah,' I say. 'We'll thrash them.'

We get the glare from Miss Roberts, and I turn my mind back to angles and gradients. It's the last lesson of the day and my head feels like it's full of cotton wool. I rest my head in my hands and feel my phone buzz with a text inside my pocket. I slide my phone out to have a look.

When I read the message I go cold inside. It's a text from Ella.

THEY KNOW. Meet me after school. THEY KNOW.

I want to talk to Ella before we get on the bus, but Sophie and her older sister are with her. When they see me, they fall silent. Sophie's sister folds her arms and glares at me. Ella's eyes meet mine for a moment, but she looks away.

My mind is racing. What does Ella's text mean? Who knows? And who knows what, exactly?

The bus pulls in at the Bird in Hand.

'Come on then,' says Billy, getting up. 'Mum's got cheesy chips ready for us.'

I grip the handle of my games kit. 'I'll meet you later on the pitch. I've got to go back home for my football boots,' I lie.

Luke frowns. 'I thought you had them.'

'Wrong ones,' I say.

Luke and Billy look at me. 'We meet at five-thirty. Thorne will go mad if anyone's late.'

I nod and stare ahead. 'I'll be there.'

The last few miles seem to take for ever. I jump off the bus at our stop and wait for it to pull away before turning to Ella.

'What's happened?'

Ella glances over her shoulder. 'They know,' she says. 'Mr Thorne told us.'

'Told you what?'

She stops to face me. 'The Birders know a tagged female hen harrier disappeared on Sunday.' She bites her lip. 'The thing is, the bird your brother shot is Storm, the school hen harrier. Mr Thorne said they've been watching her on Kingsmoor for weeks. It's been completely top secret, that's why none of us knew.'

I feel my mouth go dry. 'So they were there, watching?'

Ella shrugs her shoulders. 'I don't know. Mr Thorne is going to talk about it at assembly tomorrow.'

I feel a little bit of hope rise up inside me. 'If they'd seen Ryan shoot Storm, the police would be around by now.'

'Maybe,' says Ella. She turns and heads up the hill. 'It's going to be in the *Evening Post* this week. Mr Thorne's written a piece for it.'

I walk behind her. That's all we need. People will point the finger at us anyway.

Ella fiddles with the strap on her school bag. 'Joe, why don't we tell Mr Thorne? We could just say we found the chick ourselves.'

'No,' I snap. 'He won't stop there. He'll use Ryan the way he used Dad. It's not just the grouse shooting. It's personal. He wants to get at us too.'

'Mum's out,' I say as we reach the cottages. 'We've got time to feed the chick. It hasn't eaten since this morning.'

We let ourselves into the shed and hear the rustle of the harrier chick on the dustsheet. Ella gets to work cutting up a day-old chick, and feeding it to the hungry harrier. It opens its mouth wide, and tries to stand on its legs. It's lost some of its grey fluff, and blue-grey stubs of feathers are pushing through its wing tips.

'D'you reckon it's a girl or a boy?' says Ella.

'Dunno,' I say. 'How can you tell?'

Ella pulls a large hardback book from her bag. 'It might say in here,' she says. 'Mr Thorne lent it to me.'

I pick up the book and turn it over in my hands. It's old and the white book jacket is covered with yellowed cellophane. It's well-thumbed too. 'Why did he lend you this?'

'I was asking him about harriers. He was only too pleased to tell me all about them.'

I drop the book as if it's hot.

'Don't worry,' says Ella. 'I'm not going to tell him about our chick.'

I wish she hadn't said anything to him. I wouldn't put it past Mr Thorne to put two and two together.

Ella picks up the book and flops over the pages until she's found the one she's looking for. She's reading it, a frown of concentration on her face. 'Have you got a torch light on your phone?'

I nod.

'I'll shine it in its eye while you hold it,' she says.

I pick up the chick. Beneath the downy feathers and soft skin, I can feel muscle and bone squirm against my fingers. It's so strong for something so small. It tries to bite the end of my thumb.

'Keep it still,' mutters Ella.

'What d'you think I'm trying to do?' I say. 'You're not the one getting eaten.'

Ella shines the light in its eye and smiles. 'I reckon it's a boy.'

'How can you tell?'

'Well,' says Ella, 'Look at the colour of his eye. In this book it says young male chicks have dark smoky-grey eyes at first, not brown ones like the females. They all turn yellow later on. And I reckon it must be about two to three weeks old. It says here they lose their fluffy down and the stubs of feathers start poking through after two weeks. The males grow brown feathers like females and only start getting grey feathers in their second year.'

'When will he fly?' I ask.

Ella flicks through the book. 'At about five or six weeks old.'

I look at the little chick. It's hard to imagine him growing so fast in that space of time.

'What if we get caught?' voices Ella. 'Sophie at school is mad about Storm disappearing.'

'What else can we do?' I say.

'I still don't understand,' says Ella. 'Why kill them?'

'They eat grouse,' I say. 'Years and years ago gamekeepers were even paid to kill them. You can't run a grouse moor with hen harriers around.'

Ella feeds the last piece of meat to the chick. 'Mr

Thorne said that only three pairs of hen harriers managed to nest in England last year. There should be more than three hundred pairs. He says it's because of grouse shooting that we have no harriers. They're still shot and poisoned by gamekeepers.'

I sigh. 'Grouse moor owners want hen harriers, but not as many. There might be a new scheme to move young harriers off the moor if there are pairs breeding close together. They call it brood management or something like that.'

Ella shakes her head. 'I read about that. It won't work. The chicks will grow up and fly back over grouse moors and be shot again, like Storm. You haven't removed the problem.'

I frown. 'It might save some of them.'

'Even if it did work and help some, there are other birds of prey that get shot and poisoned,' says Ella. 'Mr Thorne told us about it. Peregrines, goshawks, red kites and buzzards have been killed. Last year an osprey was found with broken legs in an illegal trap. And eight golden eagles went missing in Scotland. They were tagged but they disappeared in the same area. It's not right. It can't be right.'

I stare down at the chick feeling my mind unravelling.

Ella presses her face against the cage. 'What shall we call him?'

'What?'

'He needs a name.'

'Harry,' I say. 'Harry the hen harrier.'

'That's boring,' says Ella.

'OK, you come up with a better one,' I say.

'It needs to be right,' she says. She's quiet for a time, both hands resting on the cage. His dark eyes stare into hers. 'If we can release him, what d'you reckon his chances are to survive?'

My silence is her answer.

'Hope,' she says at last. 'We'll have to call him Hope.'

CHAPTER 18

Mr Thorne takes the stage at assembly. He waits for everyone to file in, tapping a piece of rolled-up paper against the lectern. His eyes travel over us and for a brief moment he looks at me. I try to shuffle behind a taller boy in front.

'Good morning,' says Mr Thorne.

Feet stop shuffling and voices repeat his words in a monotone unison reply.

He waits for silence. 'I have sad news. Some of you may have heard that another hen harrier has disappeared. That hen harrier is Storm, the female we named at this school five years ago.' He unrolls his piece of paper to show a photo of Storm. 'I know that many of you will be devastated by this loss. We have followed Storm from the moment she was fitted with a satellite tag at five weeks old. Sadly, she has become another statistic of missing hen harriers on grouse moors.'

I see Sophie glaring at me, from along the row.

'This summer, Storm returned to these moors to breed. Volunteers have been watching her nest 24/7. She had three healthy chicks.'

I feel myself going red and tuck my chin against my chest to hide my face. What if he's about to say he saw me there the day Storm was shot. I hold my breath and feel a line of sweat trickle down my back.

'Unfortunately,' Mr Thorne continues, 'we were hampered by bad luck. The volunteer who was on watch last Sunday had been ill and no one was watching the nest when Storm disappeared.'

I feel relief flood through me, but keep my eyes fixed on the ground. I don't want Mr Thorne to see my face.

'If anyone has any information about Storm's disappearance and that of her three chicks, would they please come forward and help the police with their enquiries. Storm's disappearance is being treated as suspicious.'

Back in our tutor room, there's a picture of Storm on the whiteboard and the word *murdered* written in red beneath. I look around to see who could have written it. Sophie catches my eye but looks away.

'Hey Joe!'

I turn around. Billy's looking furious. At first I think he's upset about the harrier too, but it's about the football.

'Where were you last night? Thorne is mad at you.'

'Something came up,' I say. The truth is, I forgot all about it after feeding Hope. It wasn't until it was too late for Mum to take me that I remembered.

'Try telling that to Thorne,' says Billy. He draws his finger across his neck. 'I reckon he's going to kill you.'

'I'm coming to the match tonight.'

'Yeah, well make sure you come back to mine on the way. We don't want to lose you.'

I nod, and when Billy's talking to someone else, I text Ella.

Football tonight. Can't meet later.

> I'm going to my dad's for the weekend.
> Back Sunday night.

OK, see you.

> Don't want to leave 😔. Can't wait till Sunday.
> See you in the shed. Let me know when you're alone. xxx

Billy's dad serves out bowls of pasta to us before the match. The pub kitchen is busy with the chef cooking for the evening so we eat in the small kitchen that Billy's family uses at the back of the pub. 'You've not got long before Mr Thorne picks you up in the minibus,' he says. 'Joe, are you coming back here after the match?'

I shake my head. 'Mr Thorne's dropping me at the bottom of our lane.'

Billy stuffs pasta in his mouth. 'We are going to thrash the Stingers.'

Luke grins. 'More like the Mingers! We won fifteen-nil last year.'

Billy snorts a laugh, spraying tomato sauce across the table.

His dad taps him on the head. 'Right, finish up and get your kit.'

I finish my pasta, trying to ignore the *Evening Post* right in front of me. The missing hen harrier is front-page news. I can't resist it, I lift the corner of the page and see a photo of Adam Thorne and an article written by him. There's also a small photo of Dad too. The image jolts me in my seat.

Billy's mum snatches the paper up. 'You don't want to read that, Joe,' she says.

I say nothing.

She clears my plate away. 'How's your mum? She seems to be working all hours everywhere. She's great to have here when we're busy.'

'She's OK.' I say. I know Billy's mum is trying to be kind.

'And Ryan?' she says, her head tilted to one side. 'We haven't seen him for a while.'

'Ryan's good,' I lie.

Billy's mum sits down opposite me. 'Look Joe. I think Billy's told you, but Dave and I are supporting Adam Thorne's Ban Grouse Shooting campaign. This isn't about you or your dad. It isn't just about hen harriers. We've been flooded twice in the past five years, and there's lots of evidence to show it's due to the intensive management of the grouse moors. Also, you know Henry Knight has his own accommodation for the guests. Both things have lost us business. Well, we want to see a change. But we don't want you to take it personally.'

I nod, but I'm not sure what I'm meant to say. Dad's life was the grouse moor. It's Ryan's now and maybe it'll be mine. But more and more people want change. They want to stop the grouse shooting. It's divided the people who live on the moors and those in the town. And I don't see how anything can ever be the same again.

'Pass, Joe! Pass!'

It's been a messy match. The Stingers have got better players than I remembered and it's not the easy game we were expecting. Luke has had his work cut out in goal as the ball keeps breaking through our defence.

We're well into the second half and it's still nil-nil. I've got the ball, but Billy is in a better position to shoot. One of the Stingers players rushes in to tackle me, so I pass the ball to Billy, but kick it too far forward and another player from their team manages to get it and take it down the pitch. I race after him. I'm faster and gaining on him. Our team is spread across the pitch and I can see the clear space for him to kick it forward. I slide in with a tackle. Even as my foot shoots forward, I know I'll hook his ankle and he'll trip, but in this moment I don't care. I just want to stop him.

The Stingers player falls, rolling over and over. He clutches his ankle, his face screwed up in pain. He couldn't make it look more dramatic if he tried.

'Foul!' The referee is running our way, holding up a yellow card. 'That was a foul.'

I glare at the Stingers player lying on the ground. 'He's putting it on.'

'It was a foul,' the referee repeats.

'Was not,' I say. I kick my boot into the mud. 'A blind person could see that.'

Mr Thorne joins us too. 'It was a foul. We play fair here, Joe.' He turns to the referee and they mutter something I can't hear. I see them nodding in agreement.

The referee turns and holds up a second yellow card, then a red card.

'You're off the pitch for the rest of the match,' says Mr Thorne.

I spin around to face him. 'What for? I've done nothing wrong.'

'For a foul and talking back,' he says.

I look at my teammates for support, but none of them look at me. We'll be one man down and there are still ten minutes to play. I turn and storm off the pitch.

'Idiot,' Billy hisses to me as I pass him.

I sit on the sidelines and watch as the Stingers player places the ball down in front of him for a free kick. The Stingers take the ball down the pitch, with our players struggling to keep up. There's a messy scramble near the far goal, but I hear the dull thwack of boot on leather and the cheers from the Stingers as the ball sails past Luke into the net.

One-nil, to the Stingers.

The last four minutes are a shambles. The Stingers' defence keeps the ball far away from their goal, and when the final whistle goes, the Stingers' players high-five each other and whoop at their victory. They haven't won a match against us for five years. My teammates walk off the pitch through the drizzling rain, their shoulders slumped, mud plastered on their kit. I wait for Billy and Luke by the minibus.

'Rubbish game,' I say.

'You lost us that match,' snaps Billy.

'I wasn't the one to let the ball into the net. I did nothing wrong.'

Luke shakes his head. 'It was a foul, Joe. Everyone could see that.'

I stare at him. 'Was not. He pretended he tripped.'

Billy glares at me. 'It was a foul. No excuse.'

'Yeah, well, if you'd played a better game I wouldn't have had to foul him,' I snap.

Billy pushes his face next to mine. 'Why is it that your family just can't follow the rules?'

I clench my fists and feel the blood rushing to my head.

But Billy's not finished. 'Another hen harrier missing. Coincidence is it? What was Ryan doing on Sunday?'

I punch him, right in the stomach, and before I know it, we're sprawling on the ground and Mr Thorne is trying to pull us apart. Billy stands up and backs away, wiping blood and spittle from the corner of his mouth.

'Sit next to me on the way back,' orders Mr Thorne.

I slump in one of front seats of the minibus, ready for a lecture that doesn't come. Mr Thorne stops at the Bird in Hand at the first drop-off. Billy whacks his kitbag against my head as he leaves the minibus. I rub the back of my head but say nothing.

As Mr Thorne pulls the minibus into the lay-by at the bottom of the track, he turns to me. 'You've got the rest of the weekend to think about what happened on and off the pitch,' he says. 'See me on Monday morning.'

I ignore him, climb off the bus, and head up the track without looking back.

I hate him.

I hate school. I never want to go back there again.

I hate Billy too.

But most of all

I hate myself.

CHAPTER 19

I head up the track, hoping that Mum and Ryan are out. I'm glad that Ella has gone away for the weekend too. I don't want to see anyone at all.

I walk over the rise of the hill and see Minty outside our cottage, holding Bramble and Bracken by their reins, while they munch the fresh grass.

'Thought you'd never come,' she says.

I look around. 'Who else is here?'

'Just me,' she says. 'Mummy wanted me to ask you if you were free to help out with a charity auction she's doing tomorrow night. She needs a few waiters to hand around drinks. I'm doing it too. Should be fun.'

'You could've just texted,' I say.

'I smashed my phone. And anyway, I came to see if you wanted a ride on the moor. I'm trying to avoid Mummy. She keeps wanting me to help her make elephant placemats.'

'Elephant placemats?'

Minty flicks a fly away with her hand. 'The charity auction is for 'Save the Elephants'. Mummy's friends and the London crowd are coming.'

'How much do we get paid?'

Minty slaps me on the arm. 'It's a charity auction, dummy. We're volunteering.'

'So it's tomorrow?'

Minty nods. 'It's a bit short notice. I meant to ask you earlier.'

I shrug my shoulders. I'll do anything to stay away from my friends at school. 'I'll do it,' I say.

Mum comes out with some lemonade for us, and a bucket of water for the ponies. 'How was the match?'

'We lost,' I say.

Mum smiles. 'Well, I'm sure you did your best.'

I don't think she'll be smiling if Mr Thorne tells her what really happened. 'Minty and me are going for a ride, is that OK?'

Mum looks at her watch. 'It's nearly eight. It's a bit late isn't it?'

'I've eaten already,' I say.

'We won't be long,' says Minty.

Mum sighs. 'OK. I might be out when you get back, so don't wait up for me.'

I finish my lemonade and go to get changed out of

my football kit. Minty lobs a spare riding hat for me and I pull it on and jump on Bramble's back. Bramble's even older than Bracken, but still as footsure, and she loves to get out on the moor. We ride bareback over Hare's Leap, with the evening sun breaking through the clouds, turning the heather to gold.

I look back down the valley to the distant houses. The bright-green rectangle of the football pitch jabs at the guilt inside me. I shouldn't have fouled, and I shouldn't have punched Billy. But it's too late now; I can't undo what I did.

'How's Satan?' I ask.

Minty pulls a face. 'Still lame. The vet thinks he's pulled a tendon. She's given him four weeks' box rest. Mummy's mad at me.'

I follow Minty single file through the long bracken. Bramble is so fat that she's easy to sit on bareback. I'm glad Ella's away and can't see me now riding out with Minty. Ella said she'd feed Hope before she left for her dad's and leave me to do the late feed. I check the time and reckon that I'll have to feed Hope at bedtime.

We let the ponies choose the pace and ride down the valley towards the ford in the oak woods. Here the stream broadens and a small footbridge rises over it. We take the ponies into the middle and let them drink and splash the water with their hooves. The dappled light dances on the water in diamond shards.

'I've got cake,' says Minty. 'It's a recipe the new chef is trying. Rose petal and pistachio.'

'Sounds weird,' I say.

We ride the ponies out of the stream, jump off them and let them graze.

Minty flumps down in the grass and I sit beside her. 'Here, try some,' she says, handing me a square of cake.

It tastes sweet and flowery, like cake with toilet cleaner.

'Like it?' she says.

I pull a face.

'Me neither,' she says, wrapping her piece up again. She pulls a long piece of grass and chews the end. 'Do you remember the first time we camped out? It was you, me, and Roo, wasn't it? We camped here, under these trees for my ninth birthday. We made a campfire just over there.'

I nod and think back to us pitching our tent and listening to a fox's screaming bark in the night. We had thought we were all alone, but Penelope Knight had made James and his friends check on us. 'James pretended to be a zombie outside our tent, didn't he?'

Minty spits the grass out. 'He was annoying even then.'

I laugh. 'We were terrified! We didn't last the night did we? We ended up putting our camp beds in the trophy room and pretending we were in Africa.'

Minty smiles. 'Sometimes I wish I could be nine again, and never grow up. D'you ever think that? Do you ever wish you were Peter Pan and could stay young for ever?'

I shrug my shoulders.

Minty lies back and looks up at the sky through the leaves and branches. 'I just want to do this, every day for ever. Just ride across the moor. No school. No exams. No worries.'

'No school would be great,' I say.

'I wish I could run this place,' says Minty.

'Maybe you will,' I say.

Minty shakes her head. 'James is the oldest, but he doesn't love it like me. The only bird he can identify is a grouse, and a dead one at that. He likes London. Hartstone's a trophy to him, like his cars and his posh suits. And Roo isn't interested. He loves his art and travel. But all I want is to be right here.'

'Me too,' I say. 'Though I think there are enough gamekeepers already at Hartstone.'

Minty sits up. 'Have you heard about the hen harrier?'

I frown and look at her. 'What d'you mean?'

'Another hen harrier disappeared on the moor, a tagged one. The police were round earlier. They think it's likely to have been shot.'

I sit up too. 'The police?'

'Yes, I heard Daddy talking to them. He was furious

about it. He said he'd do anything to help them find who did it.'

I curl a blade of grass around my finger and stare at the green veins on the leaf. 'Do they know what happened?'

'No,' says Minty, 'but they're investigating on the moor right now. Jolly Jackson reckons it could have been taken by a fox, and that's why the transmitter stopped working.' Minty pauses, picks up a stone and skims it across the stream, watching it bounce twice before sinking under. 'I wouldn't say this to anyone else, but Jolly Jackson's hiding something. You know how when people tell lies, they give too many details, like they've thought something through a bit too much? Well, Jolly's being like that. Then he and Daddy were in the office for ages. I asked Daddy, but he wouldn't tell me. There's something he's trying to hide.'

I stare at the ripples in the water, not trusting myself to speak in case I give away the lies as well.

I try to change the subject. 'Are there many people coming to the charity auction?'

Minty leans back on her elbows. 'Loads,' she says. 'There's a famous wildlife photographer coming to give a speech about elephants and then there's some cool stuff donated for the auction; a painting by some top artist and even a private safari holiday. It's so shocking when you read about it. In just the last ten years, over a third of the

154

African elephants have been wiped out by poachers. Just imagine if elephants became extinct in our lifetime?'

'It's crazy,' I say.

Minty pulls a face. 'It's sick. I don't know how people can shoot them.'

'What time do you want me over tomorrow?' I ask.

'About six. Oh heck,' she says, glancing at her watch. 'I'm meant to be home in ten minutes. Mummy's serving drinks for some friends and she wants me to be there. Ugh, and I don't have my phone.'

'Borrow mine,' I say. 'I'll get the ponies.'

Bracken and Bramble have wandered off into a glade of bright sunlight where fresh grass is growing, thick and tall. I grab their reins and lead them back to the stream.

Minty is scrolling through my phone when I arrive. She looks up at me hand on hip. 'You and Ella seem to be getting along well. I thought you didn't like her.'

I frown and put my hand out for my phone.

'There are lots of texts: "Don't want to leave. Can't wait till Sunday. See you in the shed. Let me know when you're alone. Kiss, kiss, kiss".'

'Give my phone back, Minty,' I say.

'Ooh. Is Ella your girlfriend?'

There's teasing but also something else in Minty's tone.

'She's just a friend. That's all,' I say.

155

'A friend you meet up with at eleven o'clock at night and six in the morning.'

'It's nothing, OK,' I snap.

'Doesn't sound like nothing to me.'

'Leave it, Minty.' I grab my phone and jump up on to Bramble.

Minty remains standing, glaring at me. I see something like fury and hurt in her eyes. 'Fine,' she says. 'Don't tell me. But it seems like Jolly Jackson's not the only one around here with secrets to hide.'

CHAPTER 20

'How was your weekend?' says Ella.

'Fine,' I say. I don't tell her about Minty reading our texts. Minty didn't speak to me all the way back on our ride and she rang to leave a message with Mum to say she didn't need my help with the charity auction after all. Her mobile's broken, so I can't contact her and I don't want to ring Henry Knight's secretary.

'How's Hope?' asks Ella.

'Come and see for yourself.'

It's Sunday evening. Mum's doing an extra shift at the pub and Ryan is watching a football match on TV. We unlock the shed and slide in.

Ella's eyes open wide. 'I can't believe how much he's grown in just two days, and I'm sure his legs weren't that yellow.'

It's true. In the week we've had him, he looks like he's

nearly doubled his size. He can almost push himself up on his legs, and when we move closer he opens his mouth and spreads his wings in defence. The feather stubs have grown longer and dark-brown feathers are breaking from their blue sheaths. He's lost a lot of fluffy down too.

'We should have taken pictures,' I say.

'Funny you should say that,' smiles Ella. 'Look what I've got.'

I watch as she pulls out a soft black case from her bag.

She opens it up. 'I told Dad I wanted to do wildlife photography so he gave me his camera. It's got all these long lenses and stuff. We've got to do a summer project and I thought I'd do one on the moor.'

A black camera body and several lenses lie cushioned against foam padding.

'Doesn't your dad need it?'

'No. He used it for motocross when he was into it. But he hardly uses it anymore. He's like that, Dad. He gets obsessed by new hobbies, gets all the kit, then drops them for the next best thing.' She pauses and gives a huge sigh. 'Mum says he treats all his girlfriends the same way.'

I turn one of the lenses over in my hands. It looks expensive. 'He just gave it to you?' I ask.

Ella nods. 'It's a guilt present. He's always trying to make it up to me, for not spending time with me.'

'Don't you want to live with him?'

Ella shrugs. 'Then Mum wouldn't have anyone.' She pauses and puts the lens carefully back in its case. 'Anyway, I wanted to get back here. I've only lived here for a few weeks, yet it feels more like home than Bristol ever did. I wanted to get back to Hope too.'

I feed a piece of food to Hope and he reaches up, and grabs my finger. 'Ow! That hurts!'

Ella laughs. 'He doesn't do that to me. I think he likes me more.'

I frown. 'I don't think he should like us at all. He'll imprint on us, like ducks and chickens do when they think humans are their parents. If he does that, we won't ever be able to set him free.'

Ella stares down at Hope. 'We're not doing this right are we?'

I shake my head.

'We've got to ask someone,' says Ella.

'We can't,' I snap. 'We're bound to be able to find out some stuff on how to do it on the Internet.'

'OK, we'll look,' says Ella. 'But if we can't I'm going to ask Mr Thorne for help. We can't let him die.'

I watch Ella feed Hope, the silence thick between us.

It was a dumb idea to try to rear this chick. We can't do it. We don't know enough. And it's all going to blow up in my face.

I almost pull a sickie on Monday morning, but I know it'll only make Mum suspicious. I wish it was the summer holidays already, but we've got two weeks to go. I climb on the bus and take a seat near the front so that I won't need to sit next to Luke or Billy. I don't even look at them when they get on. I can't skip school, because my tutor would find out at registration and ring home.

I'm trapped. I'm trapped in school and in a room with Mr Thorne about to rip into me.

I sit at a desk, fold my arms, and stare straight ahead.

Mr Thorne clears his throat. 'Have you had time to think things over since Friday?'

I say nothing. I'm not grovelling to him.

He looks at me over his large beaked nose. 'You let the football club down,' he says. 'And you let your teammates down.'

I look out of the window, at the huge clouds, and a lone bird, high, high in the sky. I watch it wheeling through the air.

I'd give anything to be that bird right now.

Mr Thorne's voice is quiet, almost a whisper. 'You let yourself down too.'

I swallow hard and try to keep my voice level. 'Have you told my mum?'

'Not yet,' says Mr Thorne. 'Maybe I won't need to. But you need to apologize to Billy.' He sighs. 'You're a talented player, Joe, but you let it go to waste. What are you going to do?'

'I'll play better against the Black Panthers,' I say.

Mr Thorne stands up, signalling the end of the meeting. 'I'm sorry Joe, but I've taken you off the team for the rest of this tournament.'

'That's not fair,' I blurt out. 'I'm the best striker.'

'I said at the beginning that it's not about talent, it's about commitment and fair play,' he says, folding his arms. 'You've missed three sessions, but Alfie Hayes has made every one.'

I watch him leave. I can't believe he's taken me off the team and hate him for it.

I avoid Billy and Luke all day and sit on my own on the bus home. Maybe this is exactly what Mr Thorne wants; to drive a wedge between everyone and our family. Billy and Luke are mad at me. Minty won't talk to me. There are people in the school who won't even look at me.

But it's not as if Mr Thorne needs to drive a wedge between Mum, and Ryan, and me. We're already breaking into pieces by ourselves.

Ryan doesn't talk to me all week. There have been Birders and police on the moor scouring the nest site. Mum's been busy with different jobs, so I've hardly seen her. She hasn't spoken about the missing hen harrier either.

Maybe she doesn't want to know. Maybe she doesn't want to go through it all again. It feels as if Mum, Ryan, and me are pulling away from each other and finding our own places to hide. I want to talk to Mum, but even she seems withdrawn, and she's so tired we never get the time. I'm not sure what I'd say anyway.

This is all my fault.

I'm betraying both of them.

I'm keeping alive the thing that could put Ryan in prison. I'm keeping alive the very thing Dad fought to destroy, and in doing so I feel I'm the one who is tearing our family apart.

It makes the decision easy.

I don't really have a choice.

We can't keep Hope here and we can't tell anyone about him. I know what I have to do. I wait until I hear Mum and Ryan are in bed asleep, and creep outside staying hidden in the deep moon-shadows. The dogs wake when they hear me and wag their tails, looking at me with bleary eyes. I glance up at Ella's bedroom and hope she's not awake too.

'Shhh dogs!' I whisper. Weasel whines but I hurry past and grab the key for the shed. My hand is shaking so much, the key rattles as I unlock the door. I slip inside and place my torch on the worktop. Its light throws Halloween shadows around the room.

Hope is asleep, but he wakes when he feels the cage moving as I slide it out into the light. He raises his head and it wobbles side to side and blinks in the brightness. His beak opens in eagerness for food, but I don't have any to give him. It's not why I'm here tonight. I'm here to put an end to our problems. I'm here to put an end to Hope.

I can't see another way.

I lift him out of the cage and place him on the floor. He backs away, lifting his talons and snatching at the air in front of me, trying to keep me away. He's so small, yet he fights so fiercely to stay alive.

I take a spade from Dad's neat line of tools. Just one blow is all it will take. Hope won't feel anything. I'll tell Ella he died overnight. It's easier this way. No one will ever know.

I raise the end of the spade above my shoulder. I feel sickened inside and my hands are shaking.

Dad's right. I am a coward.

I take a deep breath and close my eyes.

And I'm back there, that day with the vixen, in the glade where we found her. Sunlight is streaming through the lattice of hazel and the long grass is beaded with dew. I see her with the wire snare looped around her russet neck. She is perfectly still, watching me with her golden eyes.

I can hear Dad's voice inside my head.

Just do it Joe.

Toughen up.

Grow up.

Man up.

I grip the handle of the spade to stop my hands from shaking.

I raise it even higher, but the vixen's eyes haunt me. They burn right through me. In them, I see the vastness of this landscape. I see the dark peaks and wooded valleys. I see the hen harrier's soaring and tumbling flight, riding invisible rivers of sky.

I hear Hope's insistent call and I open my eyes.

This is his world.

He belongs to his wild.

He belongs to his sky.

It is not for me to take it.

I feel my heartbeat slow, and lower the spade gently to the ground.

I can't kill him.

Because I know now, that to kill him would be cowardice.

I feel hot tears sliding down my face. I sink on to the floor and curl into a ball and sob, because to let him live will take courage and I'm not sure I have enough of it inside.

CHAPTER 21

'Joe!' Mum is knocking on my bedroom door. 'Ella's downstairs. She wants to see you.'

I look at my clock. I've slept in. It's nearly nine already. I pull on jeans and a T-shirt and head down to the kitchen. I'm surprised to find that Ryan is still home. I can hear him in the boot room muttering and ransacking drawers.

Ella is standing by the sink, a rucksack over her shoulder and her camera case around her neck.

Mum smiles at her. 'D'you want breakfast? I can do some eggs.'

'I'm OK,' says Ella. She looks at me and tips her head towards the window. 'I'm going out on the moor today. D'you want to come?'

I can see there's urgency in her eyes. 'OK,' I say. 'Give me a minute.'

'Joe,' says Mum. 'You haven't seen the key to the shed have you? Ryan wants it.'

I glance at Ella and shake my head. 'What does he want it for?'

'Jolly phoned to say the police are checking all the barns and outbuildings. They might come here.'

Her voice is casual but I know what she's thinking. I'm thinking it too. Dad kept lots of bottles of old poisons from years back. I don't think he ever used them, but it wouldn't look good if the police found them here. Ryan will want to throw them all out before the police arrive.

There's a smash of glass from the boot room and Ryan curses loudly.

Mum opens the door wide. 'Ryan, what are you doing?'

Ryan looks up from picking up pieces of broken bottle from the floor, an emptied bin beside him. 'Did the rubbish go out last week?'

'What?' says Mum.

'The rubbish?' Ryan starts rummaging through another bin bag. 'Did you put it out?'

Mum shakes her head. 'There's another bag outside. Have you lost something?'

Ryan leaves the room and I can see him through the window searching in the bin outside. I put two and two together. The police are on their way and the satellite tag is inside that bin. Ryan will want to get it as far away from here as possible. Ryan knots the bin bag and puts it in the boot of the car. He sticks his head around the door. 'I'm going out.'

'Ryan!' calls Mum. 'Ryan . . .!' But Ryan has already gone. I hear the engine rev up and see him heading down the track.

Mum looks at me now. 'What was that all about?'

I shrug my shoulders.

Mum sighs. 'We'd better find the key to let the police in the shed. There's a spare somewhere in here.'

Ella pulls me out of the boot room into the kitchen. 'We've got to get Hope out of there,' whispers Ella.

'I know,' I say, 'but where?'

'That's what I was coming to tell you,' she says. 'But I haven't got time to explain.'

'Mum will see us,' I say.

'Distract her,' says Ella. 'Keep her busy until I can grab Hope and get away up Hare's Leap.'

'But Ella . . . '

Ella shakes her head. 'Later. We haven't much time.'

I go back into the boot room to see Mum on her hands and knees picking up pieces of glass. 'Where's Ella?' says Mum.

'Gone home to get something,' I lie. 'D'you want some help?'

Mum pushes back some stray hairs. 'There's glass everywhere. We don't want the dogs cutting their pads.'

I kneel down with Mum looking for pieces of glass, pretending I can see pieces to keep us looking longer.

'I think that's about it,' says Mum. She turns her attention to one of the drawers and pulls out an old biscuit tin, labelled in her handwriting, 'Tin of Lost Things'. She opens it and I see lots of keys inside; padlock keys, window keys, rusty keys to doors that no longer exist. There are old receipts wrapped in elastic bands and a broken pair of reading glasses. 'It must be somewhere,' she mutters.

I stand up and see the figures of Ella and Weasel heading along the Hare's track.

'Why don't I check around the shed,' I say. 'Maybe the key has been dropped or maybe there's a spare one hidden somewhere?'

'Good idea,' says Mum, still rummaging in the tin.

I slip into the shed and check around. Ella's tidied up really quickly. She's even swept away our dusty footprints. I leave the door open and go back inside to Mum. 'Found it,' I yell. 'There was a spare one around the back. I've unlocked the door and left it open.'

Mum gets up and brushes her knees. 'Thank goodness for that.'

I've got to go,' I say. 'Ella's gone ahead without me. I'll catch her up.'

Mum nods but looks distracted and so I slip out of the door. As I jog along Hare's track I hear Ryan driving back up the lane. I can feel sweat on my brow but it's not from running. I can't even imagine what Ryan would have done if he'd found a harrier chick in Dad's shed, and I know I don't want to find out.

CHAPTER 22

I catch up with Ella on a path over Hare's Leap Hill.
She's sitting down breathing into her inhaler.

I sit next to her and lift the sheet she's used to cover
Hope's cage. Hope looks at me from big wide eyes. He's
panting and his wings are splayed open, the long flight
feathers pushing through the bars. I don't know if it's
because he's hot or stressed but he doesn't look great.

'Where are we going?' I say.

'To Dead Man's Wood,' says Ella. 'Come on,' she says,
standing up. 'I'll tell you as we walk.'

I offer to carry the cage to give Ella a break and
we make a beeline over the heather towards the dark
rectangular patch of conifers.

'I couldn't find any information on rearing hen harriers,'
says Ella, 'and when I started asking Mr Thorne how to
do it, pretending it was for a project, he got all suspicious.'

170

'You didn't tell him, did you?'

'No.' said Ella. 'But I don't think he would have told me. He said it was complicated and difficult and best left to the experts. So I looked online and found out how to rear red kites and release them. Once they can make enough of their own body heat, they need to go to a pen where they can see their environment but they can't see us. Hope's ready for that now. I reckon we can hide him in the conifer forest. No one will see him there.'

I nod. 'As long as we keep him away from the fox snares. Ryan checks them every day.'

We take turns carrying the cage until we reach the edge of the trees.

'This cage is a bit small, isn't it?' I say.

Ella nods. 'I thought we could use the Larsen trap.' She points to the trap with its lone crow sitting on a perch.

'Ryan will notice it's missing,' I say.

'If he asks, you could tell him Jolly moved it.'

I nod. It's risky but worth a try. We need a bigger cage for Hope to spread his wings and the Larsen trap is just the size.

I walk with Ella to the trap, scanning the hill to make sure no one is watching. The crow inside eyes us warily, edging to the far side of the cage. Ella unclips the side door, opens it wide, and stands back.

'Go on,' urges Ella. 'Shoo. You're free to go.'

The crow ruffles its feathers and turns its head from side to side viewing the open space suspiciously. It slides its feet across the perch and sticks its beak outside looking up at the sky as if trying to work out its escape route.

Ella claps her hands. 'Go!'

In a flurry of wing-beats, the crow launches upwards, leaving only its musty scent behind. We watch it fly up over the dark line of trees, cawing loudly. Another crow rises up to join it and they wheel away, twisting and tumbling in the air, until they are two tiny black dots in the sky.

I catch Ella grinning madly.

'What?' I say.

'What d'you think it feels like, to be that crow?' she says.

I roll my eyes. I'm not in the mood for Ella's questions. 'Come on,' I say. 'We'll have to get this trap moved before anyone sees us.'

It takes us at least half an hour to pull and drag the Larsen trap beneath the conifers. We pull it deep into the cover of the trees so that no one can see it from the outside.

'We have to cover it now,' says Ella, 'with branches and sticks so that Hope can't see us either. We can't let him see us from now on.'

Weasel rushes around us as we collect twigs and sticks. I go deep into the wood and drag out branches, dry and brittle with age. By the time we've finished, the cage is camouflaged within the forest. We leave one end uncovered so that Hope can see the moors and landscape beyond the trees. Ella covers one end of the cage with her coat, tucking it around the edges. 'He'll die if he gets wet and cold.'

I look at her. For someone who knew nothing about these birds when she arrived, she's found out more than me.

'Let's put him in,' I say.

Ella nods. 'I've got some food for him, but we'll need to bring more tomorrow. Now he's four weeks old, we'll need to feed him several times a day.'

'We can't when we're at school,' I say.

She frowns. 'I know. We'll just have to do it when we can.'

We lower Hope into his new cage and he backs away into the corner, still fighting, still trying to take a chunk out of our fingers and trying to claw us with his talons. Ella fills a bowl with water and I chop up his food and watch as Hope picks the pieces up from the floor and feeds himself. He looks more like an adult now. Clumps of fuzzy grey fluff cling to his head, back, and legs. After feeding he shakes himself and stretches out his wings, giving them a test flap. They seem impossibly long, the tips of the flight feathers almost touching both sides of the Larsen trap. He folds them up, the feathers sliding neatly across each other, and shakes again, scratching at the fluff on his head with his foot.

'Right,' says Ella. 'We can't let him see us again. We have to stay behind the screen of branches, and drop his food and water in through the side.'

I nod and we lay more twigs and branches, hiding us from view.

Ella smiles. 'He's going to make it now. I know he is. No one will find him here.'

I'm about to say something, but Weasel growls and I see her hackles rise. She's standing rigid, looking intently at something at the edge of the wood. She sniffs the air, trying to catch the scent, but there is no wind today. Weasel steps forward, her body stiffened and tense.

I swallow hard and try to slide into the shadows, feeling we are being watched.

A figure steps out from behind the trees, silhouetted against the glare of sunlight beyond the conifers.

I try to grab Weasel and hold her muzzle to be quiet, but she bounds forward, barking furiously.

There's nothing we can do.

It's all over.

We've been seen.

CHAPTER 23

Weasel stops just in front of the figure, but then I see her tail wagging so hard that her whole back end is swinging from side to side. The figure bends down to stroke her.

I step forward through the trees. 'Minty . . . is that you?'

I can see her now, the light catching the side of her face. 'What are you doing here?'

Minty stands up straight. 'I could ask you the same thing.'

I walk towards her and hear Ella's feet sliding on the pine needles behind me. 'Just out walking,' I say. 'Ella's doing a photography project.'

Minty snorts a laugh and glances between me and Ella. 'Sure! Sure you are!'

'It's nothing,' I say. 'Anyway, what are you doing following us?'

'I saw you dragging a cage into the woods,' says Minty. She narrows her eyes and starts walking past us. 'The police are out on the moors today. Maybe they'd be interested.'

'Wait,' I say, trying to block her path. 'There's nothing, really.'

'Really?' Minty sidesteps me and walks deeper into the trees. She stops beside the cage and crouches down, pulling the sticks away. I glance at Ella and she looks at me as if I know what I should do next, but I have no idea.

Minty just stares inside the cage for some time, then gets up, replacing the screen of camouflage carefully. 'Is that what I think it is?' she says slowly.

I say nothing but glance at Ella.

'It's a hen harrier, isn't it?' says Minty.

I still say nothing.

Minty glares at me. 'It's a hen harrier chick and you stole it from its nest.'

'No,' I say. 'I didn't. I found it. Well, Weasel found it.'

Minty puts her hands on her hips. 'I'm sure Daddy will want to hear about this.'

I grab Minty's arm. 'Don't,' I say. 'Please don't. It's complicated.'

Minty pulls her arm away and just glares at me. 'There's a hen harrier missing on the moor and an empty nest. And *you* know something about it.'

'I know,' I say. 'But I can't tell you. It's secret.'

Minty glares at Ella. 'But *she's* allowed to know is she? You don't trust me any more?'

'It's not that,' I say.

'I'm going back right now,' says Minty. 'I'm going to tell Daddy.'

I watch her turn and walk away through the trees. I don't know what to do to stop her. 'OK, I'll tell you,' I shout.

Minty stops walking. She stands perfectly still, but I can tell she's listening.

I take two steps towards her. 'Ryan shot the missing hen harrier.'

There. I've said it. It's out now.

Minty turns slowly to look at me.

'Look,' I say. 'Weasel brought back one of the chicks. Me and Ella are trying to look after it and release it on the moor.'

Minty puts her hand on her hip. 'Your brother killed the hen harrier? After what happened to your dad?' She's shaking her head. 'My father will be furious when he finds out another of his gamekeepers killed a hen harrier.'

It's my turn to be furious. I stride towards her. 'Come off it, Minty. Your father knows hen harriers are killed by gamekeepers. He owns the flippin' grouse moor.'

Minty backs away from me. 'How dare you. Daddy wouldn't let it happen. I heard him telling the police.'

I laugh, even though it's not funny. 'He's hardly going to admit it, is he?'

'It's true,' says Ella. 'Your father doesn't want hen harriers on the moor. All he wants is loads of grouse.'

Minty turns on her. 'And what would *you* know? Our grouse moors protect loads of wildlife.'

'No they don't,' says Ella.

Minty looks at her as if she's something unpleasant on her shoe.

'They don't,' says Ella again. 'Grouse moors damage the land.'

'Rubbish,' spits Minty. 'These grouse moors have been here for hundreds of years.'

'Exactly,' says Ella. 'Only heather is allowed to grow here, just to keep grouse numbers up so people can shoot them. The heather is burned and burned so that the new shoots can feed the grouse. But burning is bad. There's a study that proves it.'

'Oh, so you're an expert now are you?' snaps Minty.

'It's true,' says Ella. 'Burning damages the blanket bog up here. Blanket bog is like our Amazon rainforest. It sucks up loads of carbon. No one thinks burning the rainforests is a good idea, do they?'

Minty's frowning at her. 'If we didn't have grouse shooting, the land would be overgrazed with sheep. Daddy said so. It'd just be sheep and grass.'

'So don't let the sheep back,' says Ella. 'Let the trees come back. Not the conifer plantations but the wildwoods.'

Minty puts her hand on her hip. 'Don't be dumb. These grouse moors protect many birds.' She counts them on the fingers of one hand. 'Such as curlew, ring ouzel, lapwing, golden plover, and skylark.'

'And . . .?' says Ella. 'What else?'

'What d'you mean, what else?'

Ella pulls herself up taller. 'Are those the only birds you can think of?'

Minty takes a step back. 'Well, they're really important.'

Ella is shaking her head. 'If you let the woodland come back, you'd have the moorland on the edges and you'd have the blanket bog on the hilltops. You'd still have your ring ouzels, and curlews, and skylarks, and you'd have so many other plants and animals as well.'

'OK, Miss Wikipedia,' says Minty, her hand on her hip. 'Name them. Name them all.'

Ella reaches into her bag for a notebook and starts leafing through the pages. 'How long have you got?' she says.

I look at the notebook in her hand and see pages and pages of lists in her neat handwriting; lists of trees, of birds, and mammals, and insects. The whole notebook is filled with writing and stuffed with loose photographs.

'Read it,' snaps Ella, flinging the notebook at her. 'Read all of it.' The notebook flies through the air towards Minty, the photographs coming loose and twirling down like autumn leaves. She glares at Minty. 'Because despite living here your entire life, you don't even know what you're talking about.'

CHAPTER 24

Minty is glaring at Ella, as if trying to work out if this is the same girl she met before.

'And another thing,' snaps Ella. 'You were wrong what you said before. Your grouse aren't healthy to eat. They're stuffed full of veterinary drugs and lead shot.' She puts her hands on her hips. 'Lead damages your brain cells. Did you know? Maybe that's why you can't see what's happening around you.'

Minty spins around and storms out of the trees. We watch her jump on Bramble and ride away. I want to follow, but Minty sets off at a fast trot and when she gets to the flat she puts Bramble into a canter.

Ella's eyes are brimming with tears. 'I shouldn't have gone off on one like that. I shouldn't have been rude either.'

I look across at her. 'I didn't know you had it in you.'

'It was a dumb thing to say,' says Ella. 'I've made it worse.'

I shrug my shoulders.

'She'll tell won't she?' says Ella.

I stare through the trees down the valley to Minty's distant figure riding across the moor. 'I don't know.'

'Of course she will,' says Ella. 'We've got to move Hope.'

'Where to?' I say. If Minty does tell, then we'll be found out anyway. Besides, this is the only place I know where no one will come.'

Ella sinks to the ground and picks at the pine needles. 'I thought we could do this, but we can't.'

I pick up Ella's notebook and start collecting all the scattered photographs. 'Minty won't tell.'

Ella scowls. 'How can you be so sure?'

'I know her,' I say. 'I've known her all my life.'

Ella gets up and brushes the pine needles from her jeans. 'Well, let's just hope you know her well enough.'

As we walk out into the light I glance through the photographs. 'These are good,' I say. 'Really good.' There are landscapes filled with dark moody clouds, and another of a curlew in flight against the heather.

'I took them the other night,' she says. Mum let me print them out on her printer.

I turn over the pages of her notebooks and see

lists and lists written in neat handwriting. 'What is all this?'

Ella opens the page at the beginning. 'These first few pages are the lists of plants and animals on a heather moorland,' she says. 'But everything after that are the animals and plants we could have if we let the wild come back. You see, we'd still have the heather, but we'd have woodland and bog and scrub and grasses. The list goes on, and on and on.'

'But Ella,' I say. 'This is moorland.'

'Only because we keep it this way,' she says. 'Just imagine for one moment, if these hills were woodland again. Countries like Norway have brought back their forests and it's brought back the wildlife, and tourists too. We'd have hen harriers and maybe even eagles.'

I stare at the pages of notes. 'Why are you so interested in all this?'

Ella shakes her head. 'Why aren't you?'

'I am,' I say. 'It's just . . . ' My voice trails off. What I want to say is that it's turned everything I thought before on its head.

We walk in silence across the moor, through knee-high heather. I try to imagine these moors re-wilded by forests of oak, ash, birch, and hazel. It's hard when the open heather landscape has been my life. I try to imagine walking in the dappled light of forests, listening to the sound of birdsong. I wonder what it would be like to glimpse golden eagles nesting near the dark peaks.

Ella stops beside a ragwort plant, peering at three caterpillars with vivid black and yellow stripes wriggling over the ragged flowers. 'What are these?'

'I dunno,' I say. 'Come on, let's get back.'

Ella waves me on. 'I want to take some photos. Go ahead. I won't be long.'

I walk home with Weasel down through the wooded clough. Should I go back to Hartstone to find Minty? Will she tell her father about Hope? I stop when I leave the shelter of the trees. A police car is parked outside our house and Mum is talking to a tall policeman. I can't see Ryan. Maybe he's in the police car already. I start running down the path, feet flying over the boulders, but by the time I get there, the police car has driven down the lane and out of sight.

I notice the shed door wide open.

Mum is in the kitchen sitting at a chair, her head in her hands.

'What did they want? Did they search the shed?'

Mum sits back in her chair. 'It wasn't the shed they wanted to search. They wanted to talk to Ryan.'

'To Ryan?'

Mum nods. 'They have evidence the hen harrier was shot. They found an empty cartridge and fresh footprints near the nest site. There were some blooded feathers there too.'

I say nothing, not daring myself to speak.

'I know it was him,' says Mum softly.

I shake my head. 'They can't convict him. There's no proof.'

Mum puts her head in her hands. 'Not yet,' she says. 'But they're getting closer. They'll do anything they can to bring him down.'

CHAPTER 25

'Where's Ryan now?' I ask.

'Hartstone Hall,' says Mum. 'Henry Knight wanted to see him.'

'When did he go?'

Mum looks at the clock. 'About half an hour ago.'

I start backing away to the door. 'I have to go.'

'Joe, stay out of this.'

'I can't,' I say. 'I can't.'

I can hear Mum calling after me, but I run out into the garden and up on to the moor track. Weasel barks from her kennel, but I keep running and don't stop until I reach the stable yard, where I stop gasping for breath.

Minty appears from behind me. 'What's going on? What are you doing here?'

'It's Ryan,' I say, between gasps. 'The police found an empty cartridge near the nest site.'

186

Minty stares at me for a moment then nods her head in the direction of Jolly Jackson's office. 'They're in there,' she says. 'I'm waiting for them to finish so I can speak to Daddy.'

Even from here we can hear raised voices.

I keep my head down and creep to the open window, keeping out of view. Minty follows and crouches down next to me.

'Who's in there?' I whisper.

'Daddy, Jolly Jackson, James, and Ryan,' says Minty.

I press myself against the wall and listen.

Henry Knight's voice comes booming out of the window. 'How can you be so stupid to leave a cartridge and footprints all over the place, Ryan? It's not looking good.'

'There's no proof,' Ryan mutters.

'Not yet,' says Henry Knight.

Jolly Jackson's reasoned voice interrupts. 'I've destroyed Ryan's boots and mine too, so the police can't match any footprints.'

'What about fingerprints on the cartridge,' snaps Henry Knight. 'Did you think about that?'

A long silence stretches out.

I hold my breath, not daring to breathe.

'I've got no choice,' says Henry Knight. 'You know the score Ryan. Any excuse and they'll want to make an example of us if there's evidence. What were you thinking of?'

Ryan's voice answers sounding strained but defiant. 'Kingsmoor is the best patch of grouse moor in England. Everyone knows it. My dad did his job to keep it that way. You can't have hen harriers on the moor. You know that, sir.'

'I know Ryan, I know,' says Henry Knight. 'But there are other ways around it.'

James's voice joins in. 'You might as well have put a photo in the *Evening Post* yourself.'

We can hear Henry Knight's feet pacing up and down inside. 'I'm going to have to suspend you Ryan, until we know the outcome.'

There's silence in the room again, then I hear the door open and slam shut and Ryan's boots upon the cobbles. I peer round to see him stride across the yard with his head down and shoulders hunched. I want to run to him, and walk beside him home, but I know he wouldn't want it. He shut me out long ago.

Minty is staring at me wide-eyed. I'm about to go when Jolly starts talking.

'He's just like his father,' says Jolly. 'A loose cannon.'

'He was a miserable git too,' says James. 'Everyone said so. He was a bit of a joke among the shooting guests. They'd make bets to see who could make him smile.'

I feel my stomach tie in knots.

'We can't risk bad publicity,' says Henry Knight. 'We're getting it already from the town. What d'you think Jolly. Do you want Ryan back?'

'I can't work with him,' says Jolly. 'I told him not to shoot the hen harrier. I said we'd deal with it another way. We could have come back and got rid of the chicks at night. I've put ice on eggs before to stop them hatching. Firing a shot is always going to cause trouble.'

Henry Knight sighs. 'He can't stay. I want keepers that are quiet and efficient. I don't want them to go picking fights.'

'What about his mother and Joe?' Jolly asks. 'Joe's a nice lad.'

'It's business, Jolly,' says Henry Knight matter-of-factly, 'and Ryan doesn't fit.'

The door opens and Minty and I press ourselves against the wall. We hear Jolly's footsteps recede across the courtyard, but Henry Knight and James turn around the wall to where we are. They stop and I see a moment of guilt in their eyes when they see me.

Henry Knight turns to his daughter. 'Araminta! What are you doing here?'

Minty gets to her feet. 'You knew all along didn't you?'

Henry Knight frowns and points to the window. 'Were you listening in?'

'You know,' snaps Minty. 'You know hen harriers are killed on the moor and you do nothing about it.'

James rolls his eyes. 'Minty you don't even know what you're talking about.'

Minty ignores James but glares at her father. 'You even encourage it.'

'That's enough,' says Henry Knight. He glances around to check that no one is listening.

I want to slide away but Minty isn't finished. 'You let Joe's dad and Ryan do the dirty work so you don't take the blame.'

Henry Knight glances at me, the colour rising in his cheeks. 'Don't be ridiculous Araminta. The hen harrier problem is complex. You wouldn't understand.'

Minty's face is red with anger. 'I wouldn't understand how loads of birds of prey are shot and poisoned on grouse moors! On *our* grouse moors?'

'Oh shut up Minty,' snaps James. 'You're just being a silly girl. Next you'll tell us you've turned vegetarian.'

Minty gives her brother such a swift kick in the shin that he doubles over clutching his leg.

Henry Knight glares between them. 'Enough, Araminta. Look, hen harriers are a problem, I don't deny that, but we can't go letting them all in.'

'You don't let any in,' shouts Minty. 'You just want to kill them all.'

Henry Knight stands between Minty and James. 'We'll talk about this later when you've calmed down.' He turns to me. 'Joe . . . ' He looks like he's choosing his words carefully. 'I'm not sure what you overheard today, but you must know that we value Ryan, as we did your father. It's a tricky situation and everyone's feeling a bit heated. I'd rather chat to Ryan before you do.'

I nod. 'I'm sorry.'

Henry Knight taps his stick the ground. 'Good lad,' he says, patting my shoulder. 'Good lad.'

I watch him walk away, following James who's rubbing his shin and glaring at Minty.

'He lied,' says Minty. 'He lied. He said he wouldn't have hen harriers killed on his moor, but he lied. I wonder how many other lies he's told.'

'I've got to go home,' I say. I want to get back and talk to Mum. I want someone to sort this whole mess out. I walk away, hands in pockets. I'm not sure what it means if Ryan has to leave. Where would we go? I can't imagine living anywhere but here.

I'm jogging back across the track when I hear hoof beats behind me.

'Joe! Wait!'

I turn to see Minty trotting along the track on Bramble.

I slow down to a walk and wait for her to catch up with me.

'I'll help,' she says.

I turn to look at her. 'What?'

'I'm in. I'll help you and Ella look after the hen harrier.'

'You didn't tell on us?' I say.

Minty looks down at her hands. 'I almost did. That's why I was waiting to speak to Daddy. But Ryan arrived. And then you came along and I heard it all. I'm sorry Joe. I don't want you to leave the moor.'

'It's a mess,' I say.

'It's not right, though, is it?' she says. 'Mummy and Daddy have charity auctions to save the elephant and here we are killing wildlife on our own land. They're such hypocrites. I don't know why I haven't seen it before.'

I shrug my shoulders. 'It's been happening for years.'

Minty shakes her head. 'There's no excuse for it. It has to stop.'

'Then you'd have to stop driven grouse shooting,' I say. 'You can't have both.'

'I know,' says Minty. 'If it were me, if I ran Hartstone, I'd do exactly that.'

CHAPTER 26

I walk the rest of the way home with Minty's words spinning in my head. What if grouse shooting could be stopped? What if the forests returned? What if we had hen harriers? What if we had eagles soaring these skies? What if? What if? What if?

They seem impossible thoughts. The moors have been a way of life for so long. Maybe that's the problem. Maybe we're too stuck in an idea of a recent past, preserved and pickled in tradition. Maybe we don't dare imagine a different future.

I find Mum sitting at the kitchen table staring into space.

'I thought you were at work,' I say.

'I phoned in to say I couldn't make it,' she says. 'Ryan's been suspended.'

I sit down opposite her. 'I know.'

Mum slams her hand on the table. 'If Ryan goes to prison, Henry Knight should go to prison too.'

'Henry Knight wants us out of here,' I say.

'What d'you mean?'

'I overheard him tell Jolly Jackson he wants us gone.'

Mum is silent, her lips drawn in a thin line. She shakes her head. 'I won't be sorry,' she says. 'I won't be sorry to leave this place. Maybe we need a fresh start somewhere away from here.'

'I'll be sorry,' I say.

Mum looks at me as if she's seeing me for the first time.

'I don't want to leave,' I say. 'This is my home.'

Mum leans forward and puts her head in her hands. 'Well, I don't think we'll have a choice. I don't think our future's here.'

I hardly sleep all night. I just keep turning over and over what will happen to us. Where will we live? Will Mum be able to get a job somewhere else? We'll have to move, maybe to a city, maybe far from here. What will happen to Ryan? What if I'm not allowed to keep Weasel? It feels like solid rock has turned to quicksand and there's nothing to hold on to. Our family's been at Hartstone for generations, but we're not wanted any more.

I'm not wanted at school either. Sophie and Lily have

taken it upon themselves to make posters of Storm and put them all around our tutor room. I keep finding pictures of dead hen harriers in my locker and left carelessly on my desk. I can't tell Mr Thorne, as he'd have no sympathy. I've got a cracking headache too, so I miss lunch and sit outside on a bench by the playing fields.

'Oi, Joe!' A football whacks the side of my head.

I spin around. Luke and Billy are walking towards me over the grass. I haven't spoken to Billy since our punch-up.

'What you doing out here?' says Luke.

I shrug my shoulders.

Billy bounces the ball against my head again. 'You not playing football?'

I rub my head. 'Thorne's banned me from the match.'

'We know,' says Luke. 'But d'you want to kick a ball about now?'

'Unless you're still being an idiot,' says Billy. He lobs the ball at my chest.

I catch it and turn it over in my hands, looking at the fine cracks in the leather. I can't even look at Billy.

He knocks the ball out of my hands. 'Come on, we've only got ten minutes before the bell.'

I get up and walk with them down to the playing fields.

I scuff the grass with my feet and glance at Billy. 'You still mad at me?'

'You cost us that match,' he says.

I push my hands deeper in my pockets. 'I know. I'm sorry.'

Billy bounces the ball in front of him, the thud echoing from the walls of the sports hall. 'I shouldn't have said what I did about Ryan,' he says. 'I'd have punched me if I were you.'

I rub my hand at the memory. 'I messed up. I wish I could play against the Black Panthers with you. It's going to be a disaster with Alfie as striker.'

Billy gives me a shove. 'I reckon we're in with a chance. Check out Alfie's footwork. We never knew he had it in him. You'd better watch out next year.'

We practise penalty shots for Luke to save, slamming the ball towards the goal. Alfie's like a different player. I watch him kick ball after ball past Luke into the net.

'What happened?' I say to Billy.

'The Stingers' ref told Alfie he had the makings of a star,' says Billy.

'And . . . ?' I say.

'Well that was it,' says Billy. 'The ref used to be a regional scout. He's the guru of self-belief. He said Alfie had the skills, he just needed some practice and someone to tell him he was good.'

I feel a tinge of jealousy inside as Alfie takes the last shot, the ball curving through the air and a massive grin on his face as it flies into the goal.

When the bell goes, we walk back into class. Sophie and Lily make a point of walking a wide berth around me.

'They'll get over it,' says Luke.

'I keep getting notes slipped in my locker with pictures of dead hen harriers,' I say.

'It's not them you should be worried about,' says Billy.

I frown. 'What d'you mean?'

It's her,' says Billy, pointing to a girl in the distance.

'Ella?' I say.

Billy nods. 'We heard her talking to Thorne this morning. She was showing him photos of hen harriers and the moor. I heard him say he's got something planned.'

'What is it?' I say.

Luke shrugs his shoulders. 'Dunno. We didn't hear. They're up to something. I'd keep a close eye on your neighbour if I were you.'

I stuff my pockets with a couple of day-old chicks from the freezer, unclip Weasel, and join Ella on the track up to the moor. Weasel bounds ahead of us, leaping through the bracken.

I look sideways at Ella. Is she really planning something I don't know about?

'Minty's meeting us up there,' I say.

Ella frowns. 'Minty? What does she want?'

'She wants to help,' I say. 'She didn't tell her father about Hope.'

Ella is silent the rest of the way. She shoves her hands deeper in her pockets when we see Minty sitting on a log, letting Bramble munch the grass.

'Hi,' says Minty.

Ella nods but walks past her into the conifer plantation.

Minty and I follow. Even though I know where Hope's cage is, it takes me a moment to find it in the darkness.

'It's really camouflaged,' says Minty. She kneels down to pull away a pine branch.

'Don't,' snaps Ella. 'He mustn't see us.'

'Sorry,' says Minty. She stands up and backs away, watching Ella.

Ella crouches down to peer through the gaps in the screen of branches and leaves. 'He's eaten all his food from yesterday.'

I pull out the chicks from my pockets. 'I've got some here.'

I brought a grouse,' says Minty. 'It was in the freezer from last year. He'll have to get used to eating stuff he can find on the moor. It's plucked and gutted, but hopefully he'll like it.' She puts it on the ground next to the day-old chicks.

'Good idea,' I say. 'We'll have to chop it into smaller pieces for now though.'

I watch Ella and Minty set to work cutting up the grouse. Ella glares at Minty before turning her back on her, and savagely sawing meat from bone. Ella slides pieces of food into the cage and we all watch through the gaps to see Hope stalk closer to the grouse and begin to pull at the loose flesh, holding it in his talons and tearing strips with his beak.

Ella wipes her hands in the grass and stands up. 'We're done,' she says. 'I've got to get back.'

'Me too,' says Minty.

We scan the landscape before leaving the conifers.

'I think we should take it in turns coming up here,' I say. 'It's going to look suspicious if we're all up here every day.'

Minty nods. 'I'm happy to do a shift.'

Ella glances at her. 'We'll be fine, thanks. We don't need help.'

'We do, Ella,' I say. 'We need all the help we can get.'

Ella looks across at Minty. 'Why are you helping us?'

Minty pushes back her hair and looks directly at Ella. 'You were right and I was wrong.'

I snort in surprise. I don't think Minty's ever admitted she was wrong to anyone.

Minty casts me a glance. 'Shut up, Joe. I mean it, Ella's right. It's not just the hen harriers. It's all of it.'

Ella picks at pine needles and rolls them between her fingers. 'You can't tell anyone about Hope,' she says. 'This has to be our secret. No one must ever know.'

Minty nods. 'I know.'

Ella frowns. 'How can we trust you?'

'I know already,' says Minty. 'If I wanted, I could go and bring in the Birders and police right now.'

'So why don't you?' says Ella. 'What's in it for you?'

'If I call in the police, Ryan will get blamed and everything at Hartstone will carry on as before,' she says. 'If you want Hope to survive, Hartstone must change. If you want Hope to survive, you need me too.'

I stand watching them, listening to the wind in the branches above and the patter of dry needles on the forest floor.

'OK,' says Ella. She stands up and brushes the pine needles from her jeans. 'Then we'll do it. We'll do it together.'

'I can do the shift when you're both at school,' says Minty.

Ella nods and we follow her out of the dark forest and into the light.

Minty pulls Bracken's head up from the patch of grass

and turns to Ella. 'Do you want to ride as far as the sheep track?'

Ella's eyes open wide. 'Really?'

Minty nods. 'See if my hat fits you.'

Ella pulls it on and smiles. 'You won't tell my mum will you?'

'I'm good at secrets,' says Minty.

She gives Ella a leg-up on to Bramble, and together we pick our way across the heather and on to the track, with Ella clinging to Bramble's mane, and me and Minty walking by her side, with Weasel bounding ahead of us.

CHAPTER 27

I'm counting down the days until the summer holidays. It's only one week to go. I can't wait. This time next Friday school will be over. It's not as if we're doing much work at school anyway. I reckon the teachers are counting down the days too.

Billy slaps me on the shoulder. 'Are you going to come and watch us practise for the match against the Panthers?'

'Not if Thorne is there,' I say.

'We hardly see him,' says Billy. 'He's getting ready for the march through town to ban grouse shooting.'

'What day's it happening?' I say.

'The twelfth of August of course,' says Luke. 'The start of the grouse-shooting season.'

'Sophie and Lily are helping him,' says Billy. 'Your neighbour is too. They've been having lunchtime meetings about it.'

202

I frown. Ella hasn't told me anything about this.

'So you coming to watch?' says Luke.

'Nah,' I say. 'I'd better get back.' The truth is I want to know what Ella's up to. I don't think she'd tell Thorne about Hope, but there's something she's not telling me. She hasn't been up to see Hope much this week, leaving Minty and me to do most of the shifts.

I climb on the bus behind Ella, but it's not until we're on the moor on our way up to see Hope that I try to find out what she's been doing.

'Where've you been all week? I've hardly seen you,' I say.

'I've been out on the moor with my camera,' says Ella. 'I saw the male hen harrier again.'

'You got photos?'

Ella nods. 'D'you want to see?' She pulls her camera from her bag and stops to show me the picture on the screen, and zooms in so close that I can see every single feather and the markings on its iris.

'It's brilliant,' I say.

'I've got others, she says, and scrolls through river scenes taken in fast exposure showing every water drop in detail, and waterfalls like suspended lace, and others taken in slow exposure, the water a blur of white. Ella has photos of a crow and a kestrel, and even a young fox trotting through dappled shade.

'I've got tons of Hope too. It's amazing to see how much he's changed.'

'What are you going to do with all these?'

Ella shrugs her shoulders and her face colours bright-pink.

I frown. 'Have you shown these to Thorne?'

'He wanted to look,' says Ella.

'You didn't show him *all* your photos?'

'Course not,' she says. 'None of Hope.'

'What does he want them for?'

'He wants to use them,' says Ella. 'He's getting some printed in A3 size and putting them up in the town hall, and using some in an article he's writing for the paper about the Ban Grouse Shooting campaign.'

I stop and face her. 'You're not just going to let him have them are you?'

'I know you don't like him, Joe,' says Ella, 'but he's trying to save the hen harriers too.'

'You're right,' I snap. 'I don't like him.'

I stride ahead of her towards Dead Man's Wood. A few weeks ago she wouldn't have been able to keep up, but I hear her behind me, matching my strides with hers.

'Can't you just let it go, Joe?' she says.

I stop and she almost crashes into me. 'Adam Thorne would put Ryan in prison if he could. I don't want anything to do with him.'

I duck under the conifer trees to Hope's cage, and peer in. Although he can't see us he can hear us and he stands up stretching his wings. The primary feathers have grown long and strong. He stretches his wings wide and flaps them, testing his strength.

'According to the book he should begin to fly this week,' says Ella. 'But we can't just let him fly off. We'll still need to feed him. When I read about the red kites they give them bigger cages to practise flying.'

'Where can we get a bigger cage?' I say.

Ella shrugs her shoulders. 'We could make one.'

'There's chicken wire in Dad's shed and some bamboo poles,' I say.

Ella nods. 'It wouldn't be for that long. Only for another three weeks until he's ready to leave at about eight weeks old.'

I look at my phone, working out the date. 'That'll be the start of the grouse-shooting season,' I say. 'The twelfth of August.' I crouch down to look at Hope and can't decide if it's an omen for good or bad luck.

Ella crouches next to me. 'We'll do it then,' she says. 'We'll set him free on the Glorious Twelfth.'

CHAPTER 28

I'm relieved when school ends for the summer. The Black Panthers won the last match of the tournament, but only by one goal. Alfie was made man of the match for fair play.

The rumours have got out that a gamekeeper from the Hartstone estate shot the hen harrier, even though nothing can be proved. The police said there was insufficient evidence to bring a prosecution, but it didn't stop the comments or looks from people. I've hardly seen Ryan since he was suspended from Hartstone. He's been in his room all week with the curtains closed, and Mum's had to take his meals to his room. Mum's worried about him, but I'm just angry. He hasn't even checked on his dogs, so it's up to me to walk and feed them and look after his ferrets. Maybe it won't be such a bad thing if we have to move from here. Maybe Mum's right; we need a new place, a new start.

At least now the holidays have started I'll have time to build a new cage by the end of the week. I collect bamboo poles and coils of chicken wire, and Minty brings a roll of fruit netting she's found at Hartstone.

I help Minty unpack the things she's brought on Bramble.

'Ella's away at her dad's for a couple of days,' I say. 'It's just us.'

Minty nods. 'We haven't got much time.'

'I reckon we'll have to nail the netting to the tree trunks and make a space big enough for Hope to practise a few flaps in.'

Minty nods. 'How big does it need to be?'

'As big as we can make it, I guess.'

I take off my coat and fold it on an old tree stump, feeling in the pockets for the box of nails. We take turns rolling out the netting and nailing it to the trees, working in silence, the only sounds the tapping of nails into the soft bark. We try to build sides and a roof out of the netting, so that Hope can't escape and that foxes can't get in.

'I've been reading up about that stuff Ella was talking about,' says Minty. 'Rewilding . . . you know, letting the woodland come back.'

'And?' I say.

Minty puts the netting on the ground and turns to

look out between the trees to the moor. 'She's right. It could change this place. People would come to see the birds of prey, and the woods, and the forests. We could run Hartstone for ecotourism. James says I'm being ridiculous, even when I showed him how the sea eagles on Scottish islands have brought in millions of pounds.'

'What about your father?'

'Daddy says we've been looking after the moors this way for generations and we're not going to stop now.' She sighs. 'If I get to run Hartstone, I'd let the wild come back. I've thought it all through,' she says with a smile. 'I'd need you here. You'd be a wildlife ranger.'

'Me?' I say and laugh. But it makes me think. Maybe in some parallel universe Weasel and I could walk these hills until we're really old. I would never need to leave. Ever. I can see the shape of Black Rock through the trees and think of Dad, because I know that's what he wanted too.

We use up all the netting, but there are still big gaps and one side is unfinished.

'I'll bring more tomorrow,' says Minty. 'We're nearly done. Hope can stretch his wings tomorrow and practise flying.'

I part ways with Minty at the sheep track and walk home, my shadow long and stretched out before me. I'll be late for supper and Mum will be mad at me. I reach for my phone, but realize I've left it in my jacket pocket in the conifers. I could leave it there until tomorrow, but I promised Ella I'd let her know how Hope is. I'll have to jog back to get it.

By the time I reach the conifers, the hill has cast its shadow over the trees. They seem even darker, more impenetrable. A shiver runs through me. There's something sinister about them, something from the old fairytales of witches and evil spirits, especially at night.

I slide under the trees and wish Ella or Minty were here too. It's a stupid thought. I was here less than an hour ago, but it feels different in here now. Even Weasel is quiet and stays close to my side, her tail tucked low. I have the uncanny feeling I am being watched and feel the hairs on the back of my neck rise. A wind hisses through the branches, lifting them and breaking up patterns of light between the trees. For a moment I think I see something slide along the trees beside me. I am being stupid. I just need to grab my jacket and go. I find the tree stump where I left it but it's not there. I'm sure I left it on this one. Maybe I'm mistaken.

'Is this what you're looking for?'

I spin around. In the half-light I see the silhouette of a man and for one brief moment it looks like Dad standing there.

'Ryan?' I say. 'What are you doing here?'

'That's what I came to ask you,' he says. 'But it seems I've found out.'

Ryan is calm. Deadly calm.

Weasel stays close by my side. 'Why did you follow me?'

'Kept seeing you heading off with pieces of wood,' he says. 'Wondered what you were up to.'

'Nothing much,' I say.

Ryan strides past me towards the cage. There's no point me trying to stop him; he's much stronger than me. He crouches down and pulls away the pine branches screening the cage from view, then turns, his eyes opening wider and wider.

'I thought you were keeping a fox cub or something.' He shakes his head. 'But a hen harrier, Joe? A hen harrier?'

I take a step towards him. 'It was the one from the nest. Weasel brought it back.'

'Weasel?' Ryan snorts a laugh. 'That dumb dog actually retrieved a bird?'

I stay silent but don't take my eyes off him.

'Who else knows?' he says.

'No one,' I lie.

Ryan stands up. 'Who else, Joe? Tell me.'

'Minty and Ella. That's all.'

Ryan pulls at the netting and I hear it rip away from

its attachments. He studies the Larsen trap. 'I wondered where this went. I thought Jolly had moved it.'

Ryan takes a swig from his hip flask and puts one hand on the bolted door of the trap.

'Don't, Ryan,' I say.

Ryan slides the small bolt and reaches in, grabbing Hope by a leg, dragging him to the opening. Hope's wings beat against the ground and the sides of the cage. Feathers fly in the air around them.

'Ryan . . . '

But Ryan pulls Hope right out and holds him upside-down by his legs. Hope's wings beat the air and he tries to tear at Ryan's hands with his beak, but he can't reach.

'Leave him!' I yell.

But Ryan holds Hope higher. 'You still don't get it, do you? Dad died because of this bird. I've lost my job because of this bird. What's left for me? No one will employ me now. I've got nowhere to go. I've got nothing, Joe. Nothing.'

Hope is becoming more frantic, twisting and turning in Ryan's grip. It wouldn't take much for Ryan to kill him.

'Put him down Ryan, please,' I beg.

Ryan takes a step closer. 'What would Dad say if he could see you now?'

I say nothing but my stomach tightens so much I feel sick.

'Dad would be ashamed of you,' sneers Ryan.

'I don't care,' I say. 'Dad hated me, anyway.'

Ryan frowns. 'He didn't hate you.'

'He did.' I take another step towards Ryan. 'He wanted me to be like you, but I was never good enough.'

'That's not true, Joe.'

'It is, and now I don't care. He wanted me to be like you, and him, and Grandad. I had to be what he wanted me to be. It's like these moors, he couldn't see them any other way either. He didn't want to.'

Ryan's shaking his head. 'Dad loved you Joe.'

'No he didn't.' I almost spit the words out. 'He hated me and now I hate him too. All my life I wanted to be like you. But not now. Not now. If you kill Hope, you'll never see me again. Ever. If you kill Hope, I'll hate you too.'

CHAPTER 29

Ryan doesn't move.

Weasel whines and presses against my leg. I don't know whether to step towards Ryan or away. His face is hidden in shadow so I can't guess what he's thinking.

He slowly lowers his hand and uncurls his fingers, letting Hope drop to the ground and scrabble away from him into the darkness of the trees.

A rush of wind hisses though the branches, and the tall trunks creak and groan above us.

I can't bear his silence. 'Ryan?' I say.

He doesn't say anything, but starts walking towards me, his feet heavy on the ground. I start to back away, but Ryan grabs me. He wraps his arms around me, all the way around. And as he holds me, I feel the sobs rack through his body. I feel his hurt; the hurt of losing Dad, the hurt

213

of losing the life he loves, and of not being what Dad wanted him to be.

I wrap my arms around him, and hold him too.

Us.

Together.

Two brothers.

For the first time in our lives it feels as if I am holding him up, and it's not him who's holding me.

Ryan lets go of me and sinks on to the ground. I sit beside him, and trace patterns in the pine needles with my fingers.

'I'm finished, Joe.' says Ryan. 'Henry Knight won't have me back.'

I nod. 'I heard.'

Ryan kicks a tree root with his foot. 'He knows he has the best grouse moor because Dad and all the keepers before him killed the harriers.'

'We're nothing to him,' I say. I glance back to see if Hope is still near the cage. 'Besides, it can't go on.'

Ryan turns to look at me. 'So you're with the Birders now?'

I flick pine needles into the air. 'It's not about us and them,' I say.

Ryan frowns. 'What is it about then?'

'It's about this place, this landscape,' I say. 'It's about what it could be.'

Ryan runs his hand through his hair. 'It's not what Dad would have wanted.'

'No,' I say. 'But just because he was our dad, doesn't mean he's right.'

Ryan takes a deep sigh. 'Dad didn't hate you.'

I say nothing.

'Funny really,' says Ryan. 'Dad used to tell me you reminded him of Nan, when she was young. She had a soft spot for foxes too. She once hid one from the hunt in the wood shed. It was the only thing she and Grandad ever argued about.'

'I never knew,' I say. And something hurts deep inside me, because I've known Nan all my life and I never really talked to her. And now it's too late, because she can't even remember who I am.

Hope hops away through the trees, and crouches under the cover of a fallen branch. 'You say Araminta Knight is helping look after this harrier?' says Ryan.

I nod. 'She brings grouse for him to eat.'

Ryan's eyebrows shoot up on his forehead. 'You're telling me, Araminta Knight is feeding her father's grouse to a bird he tries to keep off his land?'

I nod. 'Yup.'

'And he knows nothing about it?'

'Minty wants to stop grouse shooting on the moor.'

'Does she now?' says Ryan. He shakes his head and

215

begins to laugh, a real belly laugh. 'Really? And will Henry Knight get to know her plans?'

I shrug my shoulders. I don't know if even Minty will be brave enough to tell him.

Ryan turns back to Hope. 'So how do you plan to look after your bird?'

I hold up the netting. 'We're trying to give him a bigger pen until he's ready to leave. Ella's got it all worked out.'

Ryan gets up and wanders around the netting I've nailed in place. He inspects it and pulls at loose pieces. 'It's not fox-proof. You'll get a fox in here and he'll be gone.' Ryan wanders around, scratching his head. 'I reckon you'll need a platform, somewhere he can get off the ground. I've seen young harriers roost in low trees. It's safer.'

'You'll help?' I say. 'Please say you'll help.'

Ryan looks at me and for the first time in a long while, I see a real smile. A smile that reminds me of when we were kids and up to no good together. 'I might as well,' he says. 'I've got nothing else to do now, have I?'

Ryan tacks down the netting, making it secure against the tree trunks. There's enough space for Hope to have some practice flights. 'We'll need more wood and wire to seal the base of the pen,' he says. 'We'll put Hope in the cage for now and come back tomorrow to finish this.'

216

'We'd better get back home,' I say. 'Mum will be wondering where we are.'

We walk back together, the setting sun bending and folding our long shadows across the contours of the hill. A memory slips in of Dad and me. I'm walking home with him, trotting to keep up with his long strides. I'm standing waist-high to him, holding the first fish I ever caught and feeling about six feet tall. I remember feeling so proud that day. But it wasn't because I'd caught the fish. It was because he'd shown me the still pools where the fish rested, pointing into the current. We'd watched the dippers flit from rock to rock and dive beneath the water looking for insects. He'd held my hand and let me in, to be a part of his world and love it too.

'It's going to be different one day,' I say.

'You reckon?' says Ryan.

I nod. 'This landscape is going to change. There'll be woodland here, all over, and moor on the fringes and blanket bog on the very tops.'

'And what will become of us in this new world of yours?' says Ryan.

'We'll be needed even more, to protect the landscape and the animals. We'll be wildlife rangers, not gamekeepers. We'll be paid to protect the wildlife, not kill it.'

'It's not that easy, Joe,' Ryan says. 'Nothing is truly

wild in this country. We'd still have to intervene. If we don't control the deer we'll be overrun with them and they'll eat the young trees.'

'But maybe we should do what they've done in countries like France, and Spain, and Germany,' I say.

'What's that?' says Ryan.

I grin. 'Bring back the wolves.'

'Wolves?' says Ryan, his eyes scanning the landscape. 'Wolves, here in England?' He shakes his head and laughs. 'Just imagine that.'

CHAPTER 30

In just two weeks we see Hope learn to fly, from the first wobbly helicopter lifts into the air, rising a few inches off the ground, to flapping from one end of the pen to the other. Once we found him with his talons caught in the netting and hanging upside down, wings beating uselessly.

Since school has finished we've met nearly every day to see Hope.

Ella peers in at him. 'D'you think he'll be ready to fly free next week?'

'We can't keep him here for ever,' I say.

Minty unzips her rucksack. 'I've been thinking,' she says. 'We have to try and train him to catch his food.'

'How?' I say. 'We can't put live birds in there.'

Minty delves into her rucksack and pulls out a roll of fishing line. 'We'll make him work for his food.'

We watch her tie one end of the fishing line to a day-old chick and push it into Hope's cage.

Ella and I watch as Minty tugs it across the ground, trailing a groove in the deep bed of pine needles.

'It's not going to work,' I say.

'Shut up, Joe.'

'It's not.'

But I'm wrong. Hope's eyes latch on to the chick, and he bobs his head up and down and side to side, watching his piece of food slide away from him.

Just when I think Ella is about to pull it right out of the cage, Hope launches upwards and dives on to the food, grasping it with his talons.

'Told you,' says Minty with a big grin on her face.

I watch Hope tear at the chick, pulling it apart and throwing back his head to swallow each mouthful, and wonder if he'll be able to catch his own prey next week.

'He's earned his supper,' says Ella.

I feel my stomach rumble. 'I'm starving too.'

Minty pats her rucksack. 'I raided chef's pantry. Let's go and eat up on the moor.'

We leave Hope in the conifers and head out across the moor. Minty and Ella ride bareback on Bramble and I follow on Bracken. Weasel bounds alongside us, glad to be on the move again. Skylarks rise and tumble in front of us and grouse scurry beneath the heather shouting their alarm call at us as we pass. We take the wide track up to the top of Sheep's Back and let Bracken and Bramble graze the rough moor grass, while we sit on the rocks with Hartstone Hall far in the valley below us. Weasel buries her nose in Minty's rucksack and runs off with a ham roll before I have chance to grab her.

'Ryan's right,' says Minty. 'Your dog is useless.'

'She's not. She's really clever,' I say. 'She worked out where the food was and got it before anyone else.'

'Well she's cleverer than you,' says Minty. 'That was your lunch.'

I spin around to find Weasel, but she's already finished the roll and licking breadcrumbs from the ground.

Minty laughs, throws me an apple and passes Ella a roll, keeping it out of range from Weasel.

'It's weird, isn't it?' says Ella. 'When you look from here down to Hartstone, we could have gone back in time and we wouldn't know. I bet nothing's changed.'

Ella's phone rings in her pocket.

I laugh. 'Yeah, like they had mobile phones then too.'

Ella reaches into her pocket, looks at the screen, and frowns. 'It's Mum. I didn't think there was signal up here.'

We watch her stand up and walk away from us, listening to her mother, her side of the conversation punctuated by *yes, no* and *really?*'

221

She slides her phone back in her pocket and walks back to us, her face knotted in a frown.

'What is it?' I say. 'Does your mum want you home?'

Ella shakes her head. 'No.' She pauses and takes her phone from her pocket again, scrolling and reading the screen. Her eyebrows rise up on her forehead.

Minty stands up. 'What's the matter?'

Ella looks at us. 'There's been a lot of interest in the article Mr Thorne wrote about banning grouse shooting. The local news team has seen my photos and wants to interview me live on the six o'clock news tomorrow evening, in the public car park on the other side of the Sheep's Back. They want a child's view on it all.'

'On TV?' I say. 'You'll be famous.'

Ella bites her lip. 'This is our chance. Why don't we do this together? I could say something as a newcomer, and Joe as a gamekeeper's son, and Minty as a landowner.'

'Did they ask for that?' I say.

Ella shakes her head. 'No. But it might work. Mum phoned to check I wanted to do it. She has to fill in a form to give me permission. She's emailed all the information and the form.'

'I'm in,' I say. 'If Mum will sign a form for me.'

Ella turns to Minty. 'And you?'

Minty twists a piece of grass around her fingers. 'I don't know.' She frowns and stares down to Hartstone

Hall, squinting as if trying to pick out people through the lattice windows. 'Mummy and Daddy would be mad at me if I did. James would probably put me on a stake and burn me as a witch.'

I can see she's trying to make a joke about it, but her eyes burn fierce with tears.

'Just do it,' says Ella.

Minty closes her eyes and squeezes them tight shut. 'I don't know. I don't think I can. They wouldn't sign a form for me to talk about it on TV, that's for sure.'

'It's worth a try,' says Ella. She taps on her phone. 'I'm forwarding the email to you now. Try and get your parents to sign the form. Don't just give up.'

'It's up to you, Minty,' I say. 'It's got to be your decision.'

I watch her walk away and stand with her back to us, staring out at Hartstone Hall. This is her home, her family seat. And I now realize this is much harder for Minty than it is for us. It's hard to challenge the way you live if life is easy. It's harder still to challenge the ones you love. It makes it difficult to choose.

Ella and I have everything to gain by wanting to ban driven grouse shooting on these moors, whereas Minty has everything to lose.

CHAPTER 31

Ella and I don't hear from Minty that evening or the next day, and she doesn't join us when we feed Hope.

'She won't do the TV interview with us, will she?' says Ella.

'I know her parents won't sign the form,' I say. 'Besides, it's not easy for her.'

Ella glances at the time on her phone. 'Two hours to go. Let's get back. Mum said she'd give us a lift.'

It doesn't seem any time at all until we are bundled into Ella's mum's car and heading to the interview. Mum had no hesitation signing the form for me. She made me put on a clean shirt though, and brushed my hair. I ruffle it up again as soon as I sit in the car. I glance sideways at Ella. She's clutching some handwritten notes, sitting up straight, and staring out of the window.

'You've made notes,' I say.

Ella nods. 'I want to work out what I want to say. There won't be much time.'

I start to feel sick inside. I haven't prepared anything. I don't even know what the questions will be. I don't even know what I really want to say.

'Maybe you should just do this on your own,' I say. 'I'll just watch.'

Ella spins around. 'Joe, you said we'd do this together.'

I nod but clench my fingers together. I don't feel any better as Ella's mum pulls into the car park and we see the TV crew waiting for us and setting up the camera.

I recognize the presenter from the TV. He looks smaller in real life, but he's friendly and he shows us where we'll be standing against the backdrop of the moor when the camera goes live. He tells us to relax and think of the interview just as a conversation. Out of the corner of my eye, I see Ella's mum giving the signed forms to another crewmember. She gives us the thumbs up, but I'm already regretting saying I would do this with Ella.

A young woman with headphones and a clipboard is herding us into position. 'Ten minutes,' she barks.

I stand beside Ella, trying to think what I want to say. I don't want the presenter to talk about Dad. I don't want to hear bad things about him. I stare at the ground and try to think of excuses to get out of doing this.

Ella nudges me in the ribs. 'Over there,' she whispers.

I follow her gaze and in the distance we see a rider on a small brown pony thundering this way, a cloud of brown dust following in their wake.

'It's Minty,' whispers Ella.

'Five minutes,' barks the clipboard woman.

Minty canters into the car park, bringing Bracken to a sliding halt.

'Sorry I'm late,' she announces, jumping from Bracken's back. She removes her riding helmet and shakes out her long hair. She looks like she did when she was ten, in her old mud-spattered jodhpurs and jumper full of holes.

Ella breaks into a wide grin. 'We thought you wouldn't make it.'

Clipboard woman consults her notes. 'It says just two kids here.'

Minty bites her lip.

Ella steps forward. 'It should be three.'

Clipboard woman frowns. 'I don't have a permission form.'

'I brought it with me,' says Minty. She pulls a form from her back pocket. 'Here,' she says. 'I'm Araminta Knight, Henry Knight's daughter.'

The interviewer's eyebrows shoot upwards. 'From Hartstone Hall?' The afternoon is turning more interesting for him already. 'It is signed?'

Minty nods.

Clipboard woman examines the form and turns to Ella's mum. 'I can't see three kids on my notes.'

Ella's mum glances at her daughter and I see a look pass between them. 'It's definitely three kids being interviewed,' she says. 'I brought the forms for Ella and Joe because I was giving them a lift.'

Clipboard woman is listening into her headphones. She nods. 'OK, stand by.'

And suddenly it's all happening really quickly.

The presenter is giving a brief introduction about where we are and why we are here. Then he turns to Ella and smiles. 'And so, Ella, we've seen your incredible photos of the moors and the animals that live here. Can you tell us what inspired you to take up photography?'

Ella looks so relaxed, yet I can see her fingers tremble as she clutches her notes, trying to remember what she wants to say. 'I haven't lived here long, but I love it here. Before I moved, I had never been out on my own. But now I've done things I never thought I'd do. I've been lost on the moors and found my way again. I've seen all sorts of animals I'd never even heard of. But looking through a camera lens really taught me to see. It's not just about the light. It's about the shadows too.'

The presenter is nodding sagely. 'And what made you decide to support the ban on driven grouse shooting?'

'Once you see your first hen harrier you never forget

it. But they're being killed on grouse moors and it has to stop.'

The presenter pulls the microphone away from Ella. 'Wonderful, thank you Ella.'

I glance at Ella. I know there is so much more she wants to say, but doesn't have the chance.

He turns towards me now and I feel sick inside.

'And Joe,' he says. 'As a gamekeeper's son, why do you support a ban?'

My mind goes blank. I don't know what to say. I don't want to mention Dad, but he's all I can think about. The silence stretches out and I can see Ella cross her fingers tightly.

'My dad . . .' I say. I pause and look out across the moor over the top of Sheep's Back to Black Rock silhouetted on the horizon. '. . . my dad loved this moor.' I feel stupid because I can feel hot tears forming and I can't stop them. I blink and blink again, knowing all this is on TV right now. 'Dad taught me to love this place too.' I swallow hard. 'He taught me to fight for it.' There's too much to say and I can't put it into words. I'm relieved when the presenter turns to Minty.

'Araminta Knight,' he says. 'Your father owns these grouse moors. What do you want to say about grouse shooting?'

I glance sideways at Minty. Her voice falters at first, but then I hear it come through, the old defiant Minty.

Minty shakes back her hair. 'My great-great-great-great-grandfather Sir William Knight used to go into Africa with his gun to shoot elephants. But we know now how wrong that is. Animals all over the world face extinction because of hunting and because we are destroying wild places.'

Minty pauses and I hear her take a deep breath.

'Here in England, we have been killing birds of prey since Sir William Knight's time. Only three pairs of hen harriers raised chicks in England last year. There should have been over three hundred pairs. We can't stay stuck in the past. Here at Hartstone we need to stop burning the moors. We need to look after the land and bring back the forests and the wildlife. I want Hartstone to have a future for wildlife and people too.'

The presenter looks like he is choosing his words carefully. 'And does your father share your views?'

Minty doesn't skip a beat. 'You would have to ask him.'

The presenter turns to the camera. 'Well it's been fascinating to hear from three young people about their views on grouse shooting. If you could sum up how you feel about it . . . ' he thrusts the microphone towards Ella.

Ella leans forward. 'It's our future, and we want to have a say in it.'

The presenter smiles. 'Thank you, and it's back to the studio.'

And it's over.

All over.

I feel so stupid. I should have prepared, like Ella and Minty.

Ella nudges me. 'What's up, Joe?'

I stare at my feet. 'I messed up.'

'What you said took guts,' says Minty, 'after all you've been through.'

I look up at her. 'You too,' I say. 'Though I'm surprised your mother or father agreed to sign the form.'

'They didn't,' says Minty.

'You lied?'

'No,' says Minty. 'The TV guy asked if it had been signed, and it had.'

I frown. 'Who signed it then?'

Minty gives a wicked laugh. 'Me.'

CHAPTER 32

The presenter is tapping on his phone, and the TV crewmembers are packing their equipment into their van. In no time at all they are ready to go, and in a spin of wheels and spray of gravel they are all gone. The car park is empty except for Ella's mum, the three of us, and Bracken.

Minty's phone rings out with a text and she stares at the screen. 'I wish I hadn't got it repaired now,' she says.

Ella looks at her. 'Is it your mum?'

Minty shakes her head, and I see tears in her eyes. 'It's Daddy. He's just seen the news. He wants to see me.'

'D'you want us to come back with you?' says Ella.

Minty looks up, tears running down her cheeks. 'Would you?'

We wave goodbye to Ella's mum and walk back with Minty towards Hartstone Hall. It isn't until we are almost in the stable yard that Ella breaks the silence. 'You did really well,' says Ella to Minty. 'I didn't get chance to say what I wanted, but you said it all.'

Minty leads Bracken into a stable and takes off her bridle. She leans her head against Bracken's neck and closes her eyes. 'Daddy wants to see me in his office.'

'Do you want us to come with you?' I say.

Minty shakes her head. 'It's OK.'

'We're here now,' says Ella. 'We'll come the rest of the way. We're in this together.'

Minty nods and we follow her into Hartstone Hall, and up the back stairs.

Patricia sees us first and opens the door of Henry Knight's office wide. Henry Knight and James are inside, sitting at the desk.

Henry Knight turns in his chair to look at us. His eyes briefly take in Ella and me, but they come to rest on Minty.

He stands up and turns the computer screen to face Minty, showing a screenshot of Minty with the presenter. 'Araminta, what on earth were you thinking?'

'We need change, Daddy,' says Minty. Her voice is defiant but high pitched. 'I meant what I said.'

'You don't know what you're talking about,' snaps Henry Knight. 'You're too young.'

Minty takes a step into his office. 'We can't go on like this.'

'Do you have any idea how we run this business?' he says. 'Do you have any idea of the amount of time and money it takes?'

'You couldn't do it without handouts,' says Minty.

Henry Knight's eyebrows shoot upwards. 'What are you talking about?'

'Well,' says Minty, raising her voice to match his. 'We get hundreds of thousands of pounds from the government for just having this land.'

'Yes,' says Henry Knight. 'To look after it and protect it.'

'Exactly,' snaps Minty. 'Protect it for what? Grouse shooting? Imagine if we used that money to protect the blanket bog. Imagine if we could bring back the forests. People would come to visit the forests and the animals. We could still run Hartstone.'

James rolls his eyes. 'We don't want the masses of the Great Unwashed roaming over this place. They'd ruin it. Besides, grouse shooting is a British tradition. It has been for over a hundred and fifty years.'

Minty's voice rises even higher. 'Tradition? A hundred and fifty years ago women didn't have the vote. A hundred and fifty years ago Roo would be in prison for being gay. Tradition doesn't make it right.'

'Oh very clever, Minty,' says James, the sourness clear in his voice. 'You have all the answers don't you?'

Minty glares at her brother. 'No James, I don't. But I'm prepared to ask the questions.'

Henry Knight shakes his head. 'It was a stupid thing to do, Minty, and you know it. You've embarrassed yourself and this family.'

'You still don't get it, do you?' says Minty. Furious tears stream down her face.

'I think you're getting a bit hysterical,' says James, stretching out his legs and folding his arms behind his head. 'Maybe you need a lie down.'

Minty screams at him. 'SHUT UP!'

Henry Knight sits back down. 'Araminta. We'll talk about this later when you have come to your senses.'

Minty glares at her father and then spins around and we follow in her wake, ushered out of the room by Patricia. Patricia closes the door and smiles, tipping her head in sympathy, yet I can tell she loves the drama unfolding in front of her.

Patricia puts a hand on my arm. 'I think James is right. Minty could do with a rest.'

'Oh bog off,' snaps Minty, pulling us with her. She strides away and we follow along the darkness of the corridor, past portraits of the Knight family past and present scowling down at us.

Minty pulls us into the trophy room and shuts the door, pressing her back against it. 'They don't listen,' she says, closing her eyes to stop the tears. 'They never listen.'

Ella steps into the centre of the room and stops, turning slowly, looking at the heads on the walls, and glass cases full of stuffed exhibits. 'It's like a museum in here. There are so many animals.'

Minty opens her eyes. 'Yup, Sir William and all those who came after him loved to shoot.'

'It's weird to think they were once living and breathing, isn't it?' says Ella. She reaches up to touch a zebra's nose and makes her way to the lion rug in front of the fireplace. 'Like this lion. Long ago his feet once touched some African grassland somewhere. Yet now he's here. Imagine him walking over to us right now.'

Minty crosses the room and kneels beside the lion rug, putting her arms around its huge head, and burying her face in its mane. 'This is Cedric.' She sits back up and strokes the lion's face, running her fingers along the soft fur of its nose. 'Roo and I gave all the animals names. We used to pretend they came to life and roamed the house when everyone had gone to bed. Cedric was my favourite. I'd ride on his back across different lands. Roo's favourite was this little bird over here,' she says getting up. She leads us to a small glass case in the corner of the room. Dust lies thick on top of the case and the bird inside looks dull, its black feathers faded with time 'Look carefully,' says Minty. 'If you let the light shine on it, you see how beautiful it is.'

I edge around to where she is standing and see the dull feathers transform. The bird has an iridescent shield of green on its chest and the black feathers of its back shine from metallic blues to fiery bronze.

Ella peers over my shoulder and eyes the brass plaque at the bottom. 'Superb Bird-of-Paradise, 1898,' she whispers. 'It's so long ago.'

We follow Minty around the cages, looking in at the animals and reading out the dates.

'Sable, 1872.'

'Kudu, 1860.'

'Cheetah, 1881.'

'Golden Eagle, 1885.'

'Osprey, 1901.'

I stop at one cage of a large bird of prey with a grouse in its talons. The bird is pale-grey, with faded black wingtips. 'Hen harrier, 1910.'

Minty and Ella stop beside me, staring in.

Minty presses her face against the case, her breath misting on the glass. 'It hasn't stopped, has it? Over a hundred years have gone by and we're still killing them.'

I walk towards another case, which is empty except for some logs and dried moss in the base. 'What's meant to be in here?'

Minty shrugs her shoulders.

Ella gives a wicked smile and turns to Minty. 'Maybe we could stuff your parents and put them in here, in their tweeds and with their shotguns. 'The Last of the Grouse Shooters.'

I glance across at Minty. I'm not sure she'll find it funny.

But Minty isn't cross, or doesn't laugh. Instead, she sighs and shakes her head. 'Mummy and Daddy won't change. They'll never stop grouse shooting here at Hartstone. How can we change anything if we can't change them?'

'But it's happening already,' says Ella.

We both turn to look at her.

'What d'you mean?' I say.

Ella smiles. 'Well, look at the three of us. We want to keep Hope alive don't we?'

I nod.

'Well,' she says. 'This is it.

Don't you see?

Right here.

Right now. We are the change.'

CHAPTER 33

When Ella and I return from Hartstone, we see a car pulled up by the cottages.

'That's Adam Thorne's car,' says Ella.

I frown. 'What's he here for?'

Ella shrugs her shoulders. 'Maybe he's seen the news.'

'Well he must be at your house. It won't be me he's come to see,' I say.

I part ways with Ella and enter our house, but freeze in the doorway. Adam Thorne *is* in our house, sitting at the table with a cup of tea. I glance at Mum and back at Mr Thorne.

'Mr Thorne wanted a word,' says Mum, pulling out a chair for me to sit down.

I sit next to him, my eyes shifting between them both.

'I owe you an apology,' he says.

I stay silent.

Mr Thorne takes a sip of tea. 'When Ella wanted to borrow books about hen harriers, I never knew you were involved too. I didn't know you wanted grouse shooting banned. I heard you on the news.'

I wrap my hands around a cup of tea and stare into the steam.

'I should have talked,' he says, 'with you, and Ryan, and your dad.'

'You hated my dad,' I say.

Mr Thorne shakes his head. 'I hated what he did. I wanted to stop him.' He frowns. 'I wanted to make an example of him.'

'You did that,' I say.

Mum pours another cup of tea for herself. 'We still get letters. Hate mail. I can't go in some shops. Ryan couldn't wait to leave school.'

Mr Thorne looks down at his hands. 'I know. I'm not proud of how I have treated you or your family. I stopped listening. We stopped talking.'

'You'd not have changed Dad's mind,' I say.

'Maybe not,' says Adam Thorne. 'But maybe we'd have talked. You and me.'

'Maybe,' I say.

We sit in silence, Mum and Mr Thorne sipping their tea. The clock ticks on the wall marking time. It was at this table that Dad heard Mr Thorne had videoed him shooting the hen harrier. It was at this table that Dad had his last breakfast with us. I glance at Mum. She looks tired, her shoulders slumped and dark circles beneath her eyes, as if all the worry of the past few months has drained her, with nothing left to give.

Mr Thorne finishes his tea and stands up to go. 'I hope we can start afresh next term,' he says. He smiles. 'Besides, we need you in the football club.'

I nod, but wonder where we'll be at the end of the summer. New town? New school?

I watch him leave. 'Do you think he knows Ryan killed the hen harrier?'

Mum shrugs her shoulders. 'I think he suspects it.'

'It makes me a criminal too, doesn't it? I was witness to the crime. I didn't tell the police.'

Mum takes a deep sigh. 'You didn't want it to happen, did you?'

I shake my head.

Mum gets up and puts the dirty mugs in the sink. 'Ryan was wrong to kill the hen harrier. Your father broke the law too. But Jolly knew and Henry Knight did too. It's not going to make any difference punishing the gamekeepers. You can get rid of one and find another. We've seen that. It's the people that let it happen, the owners and managers of the moors that need to be brought to justice. That's how to stop it.'

'Henry Knight lied to the police,' I say.

'Well maybe he'll see things another way now. Not all moor owners allow hen harriers to be shot. Maybe it's a few bad apples.'

'Maybe,' I say. 'But if it is, a few bad apples are doing a lot of damage. Only three pairs of hen harriers nested in England last year. There should be more than three hundred.'

'Besides,' says Mum. She pauses and smiles. 'I hear you are helping the hen harrier population.'

I frown. 'Who told you?'

'Ryan,' says Mum. 'We had a long chat about it last night. It's been a while since we've talked.'

'What did he say?'

Mum smiles. 'He admires you. He said you've got guts.'

'Did he?'

Mum nods. 'He said you're going to need it too. There're a lot of gamekeepers and moor owners who will disagree with you.'

I stare out of the window. 'We're going to release Hope in two days time.'

'And I'm joining the march through town then too,' says Mum.

I look at her. 'Is that wise? What if someone from Hartstone sees you? Henry Knight will want us out of here.'

Mum reaches into a drawer for a white envelope. 'He already does. We have to be out by the end of the month.'

I stare at the envelope. 'So soon?'

Mum nods. 'Jolly dropped it round earlier. He wanted to deliver it himself. He was upset about it.'

'But he didn't want Ryan back.'

'I know,' says Mum. 'He couldn't work with him. He'd wanted it to work out.'

'Where will we go?'

Mum shrugs her shoulders. 'I don't know. My sister said we could stay with her for a while until I find work.'

'But that's miles away, on the other side of the country.'

'Ryan might move away, then it'll be just you and me and you'll be off one day too.'

I look around the room. 'Where's Ryan now?'

Mum shrugs her shoulders. 'He left late last night. A job interview, apparently. He won't even tell me about it. He said he'd be a couple of days. Maybe he'll tell us when he comes back.'

'But this is home,' I say. 'This is where I want to stay. I don't want to go.'

'One day you'll want more than this, Joe.'

I say nothing because deep inside, I know that wherever we go, this place will always be my home.

Like Dad.

It's in my blood.

It's in my DNA.

It's in my soul.

CHAPTER 34

I'm awake before the alarm. I've hardly slept all night, waking and sleeping and watching the clock pass through the hours until 3.00 a.m.

It's the twelfth of August.

The Glorious Twelfth.

The first day of the grouse-shooting season.

It's the day we release Hope and set him free.

I can hear Ryan getting up in the next room and I pad down the stairs. Mum is already grilling bacon and heating bread rolls for breakfast. I hear a soft knock on the door and Ella and her mum come in.

'Bacon roll, anyone?' says Mum.

'Wouldn't say no,' says Mandy.

Ryan joins us and squints out of the window into the darkness. 'We'd best not be too long. Jolly might be out and about early this morning.'

We sit there in the kitchen wrapped in warm coats and conspiracy, munching bacon rolls. It turns out that Ella told her mum about Hope weeks ago, and that's the only reason she's been allowed to come out on to the moors every day with me. But no one else knows except the five of us in this room and Minty.

Ryan arrived home late last night after I'd gone to bed. I want to ask him about his job interview, but not in front of Ella and her mum.

'Are we ready then?' says Ryan.

I nod.

Mum and Mandy watch us from the doorway, the light silhouetting their waving figures.

We leave Weasel in her kennel and walk out across the moor beneath a sky speckled with stars. It's been a clear night and the air is cold and sharp. Dew lies heavy on the ground. We don't use the torch until we're beneath the conifers of Dead Man's Wood. Minty is already waiting for us beside Hope's cage. We don't have a box to carry him, but we wrap him in a towel, covering his head to calm him. I hold him against me and feel the tension in his body and his talons trying to claw through the material.

'Let's go,' says Minty. 'We don't want to be seen.' We head out of the trees, but I turn to see Ryan hasn't followed.

'Ryan?' I call out. I duck under the trees to find him. My torch beam picks him up sitting by the cage.

'Are you coming?'

'You go on,' he says. 'I'll clear all this away. We don't want anyone seeing this or following Hope if he comes back here.'

'What happened yesterday? Where'd you go?'

Ryan sighs. 'There's a job in Scotland, on a deer estate. Jolly Jackson gave me a good reference. It's mine if I want the job.'

'And do you?'

'I can't stay here, Joe. And I can't work in an office that's for sure.'

'So you're leaving?'

Ryan nods. 'I need a new start, Joe. It's what I want.'

I feel a tightness in my chest. I've got my brother back after all these years and now I'm going to lose him again.

'I don't want you to go,' I say.

Ryan gets up and wraps his arms around me, so I'm held in his bear-like hug. 'You can visit anytime,' he says. 'There's no driven grouse shooting. They're doing what you were talking about, planting trees, and bringing back the forests. There's eagles and peregrines. Hen harriers too.' He ruffles my hair. 'You'd love it, Joe.'

I close my eyes and stay like that, pressed against his chest, breathing in the smell of him, my brother. Hope is held safe between us, and I know I'll remember this moment for ever.

'Go on,' says Ryan, 'catch up with the others. You've not got long.'

I turn and thread my way through the trees to join Minty and Ella.

I follow them single file across the moor, a pale crescent moon lighting our way. The shape of Black Rock is silhouetted against the sky. I haven't been back since scattering Dad's ashes.

I fall in behind Minty and Ella, letting them walk ahead. Below us, the lights of Hartstone are blazing, as the kitchens get ready for the first day of the shooting season. Far in the valley, car headlights weave their way between the clustered lights of the towns. But up here, we are wrapped in the dark silence of moors.

I hold Hope against my chest, my arms folded around his body, aware that is the last time I will hold him. Maybe the last time I will see him. I feel his loss already, like an emptiness inside.

This is the bird that tore our family apart and mended it again, the bird that taught me what it is to be brave. The bird that taught me what it is to be me. I long for Dad to see this too.

I want to walk beside him one more time, and see his huge frame striding through the heather. I want to make peace with him, and tell him that he taught me to love this place. I want to thank him for it.

I need to tell him that I love him.

I stop and turn, hoping to see him in the shape of the rocks or in the deep shadows, but the moors hold their secrets and are silent to me. Yet, Dad's words no longer haunt me. Maybe we have made our peace between us.

A sliver of dawn breaks on the horizon and a light wind whispers over the heather. By the time we reach Black Rock, the sky has paled and a golden sun is brimming over the distant hills.

I sit on the ground, and slowly unwrap the towel covering Hope, keeping my hands around his wings. I can feel his whole body tense, his head moving side to side and up and down, taking in this landscape, searching his sky.

'This is it,' says Ella.

I nod. This is the moment we have been waiting for, but now I don't want to let him go. His chances are so slim. We all know that.

Minty crouches down next to me. 'I wish we could have fitted him with a satellite tag. Then we could be sure what happens to him.'

'Maybe it's better this way,' I say.

Minty looks at me, and frowns. 'How?'

'Well, this way, every hen harrier we see could be Hope. We'll want to protect them all, not just him,' I say.

Ella stands facing the moor. 'I wish we could release him somewhere else. Somewhere he'll be safe.'

'It'll be the same anywhere,' I say. 'Even if Hope's released far from here, he still might return to a grouse moor.'

Minty swallows hard. 'Let's do it.'

I hold Hope between my hands, and try to stop them trembling. 'Do I just throw him up in the air?'

Ella shakes her head. 'I reckon he wants to feel safe on the ground first. Let him take his time.'

I nod. 'OK.' I shuffle forward to a patch of bare ground at the top of Black Rock.

'Wait,' says Ella. 'We have to do this together. We have to swear an oath.'

I wait for Ella and Minty to crouch beside me.

Minty spits on her hand and then places it against Hope's side. 'I swear to do all I can to keep Hope alive.'

Ella spits on her hand. 'Me too.'

I spit on mine. 'And me.'

Together we place Hope on the ground and stand back, watching.

Hope ruffles his feathers, sending small motes of golden dust into the air. He looks wilder and fiercer out here, a tiny part of this vast landscape. It's hard to believe I held him in the palm of my hand only six weeks ago. Now he's fully grown, with only the last few feathers of downy chick fluff on the top of his head. He turns on his long yellow legs to face the wind and he scans the moor. His wings open and he feels for the wind, testing its power. He doesn't even look at us. His eyes are focused on the folds and lines of the landscape.

I hold my breath.

The odds are stacked against him to survive.

He takes a few wobbly test hops, flapping hard, his legs dangling inches from the ground. Then, in a gust of wind and a single wing-beat, he lifts up into the air. For a brief moment we see the barred pattern of his underwings, and he twists away, rising and falling with the breeze, hugging the contours of the hill.

I feel an ache burn in my chest, an imprint of his fierceness left deep inside.

And he is gone

Carrying our wild, impossible dream

For him to live

To fly free

And dance across his wilderness of sky.

Dear Reader

Sky Dancer was an important book for me to write because the inspiration behind the story and my research around the topics completely changed the way I see and think about the landscape of Britain.

As children, we are curious and inquisitive. The word 'why?' features strongly in our language. We find one answer and follow it with another 'why?', and another. We become frustrated when we are fobbed off with 'because I told you so.' However, as adults we often become more accepting of facts and lose our ability to deeply question. For many years I wondered about the burning of heather on moorland. It seemed so counter-intuitive when all around the world the slash-and-burn practices in places such as the Amazon and Indonesian rainforests are condemned for destroying wild habitats and increasing greenhouse gases. What made burning the land in Britain so very different? When I tried to look for answers I read that heather is traditionally burned to 'produce a mosaic of young and old heather to provide food, shelter and nesting areas for grouse.' The answer was unsatisfactory to me, but I accepted the answer. I didn't challenge it. I didn't follow it up with another 'why?'

It has only been recently that I have begun to dig deeper, to search for answers to my questions. What I discovered helped inspire this book.

The British landscape was once a largely forested land where animals such as bears and wolves roamed. Hunter gatherers began to settle; they cleared land for grazing, and used timber for fuel and building materials. Deforestation has continued throughout history, and the bare uplands are now so imprinted into our collective memory that we regard them as wild, rugged, and beautiful. Whereas, if we could compare them to the landscapes they have been or could be, we would see them as open, treeless, and comparatively barren. Rewilding in other north European countries has shown that forests can return remarkably quickly, and the landscapes have become mixed habitats of forest, heath, and bog, rich in wildlife. Rewilding benefits humans too; upland bog and forests have huge capacity for carbon capture; forests stabilize soils and control the flow of water, helping to reduce flood risk downstream. Trees are filters for cleaner water and air. Well-managed ecotourism is a significant boost for local economies. Rewilding would also re-engage people with the natural world.

Today, much of the scenery in the uplands of Britain contains vast tracts of heather moorland. This is intensively managed for the sole purpose of rearing large numbers of grouse for people to shoot. You only have to look at Google Maps of the Peak District and the North Yorkshire Moors to see the patchwork strips of fire-scorched land and heather regrowth in this unnatural landscape. Driven grouse shooting gained popularity in the mid nineteenth century. It is and always has been a sport of the wealthy. However, burning sensitive peatland habitats has detrimental impact—they become drier and the vegetation shifts from bog to heather dominated. Water quality is adversely affected and the way water runs off the hill is changed, which may increase the likelihood of floods downstream.

Gamekeepers were once paid to shoot and trap birds of prey. Since the Protection of Birds Act 1954 the killing of all wild birds has been illegal (with the exception of game birds and some bird species that prey on them). Some predators are killed legally—foxes, crows, stoats, and weasels. Others, including protected birds of prey and mammals are illegally shot, trapped, and poisoned in high levels, particularly on some driven grouse moors. People who support driven grouse shooting want to limit the number of hen harriers on moors by removing chicks and rearing them in other parts of the country (so called Brood Management Scheme). However, it is not just hen harriers that are persecuted; eagles, red kites, buzzards, goshawks, short-eared owl, and peregrine have all been victims.

The natural world is under threat as never before. The biggest threat is loss of habitat and resulting loss of biodiversity. The UK State of Nature Report 2016 reveals that British wildlife is in serious decline. We need to reverse these changes. We need to act now. One of things we could do is put aside more places where nature is allowed to flourish in all its glory. Imagine how different some of our hills and moors could be if habitats were restored and then left to their own devices—places where predators and prey were in balance, free from trapping, poisoning, and killing. The very thought of this raises so many questions—not least how much human intervention there should be in creating wild habitats—but these questions should be encouraged and explored, debated, and studied. And who knows, maybe Britain will embrace rewilding as many of our European neighbours have done.

Sky Dancer is a story about children who dare to question what it means for the landscape around us to be truly wild. It is about children who challenge tradition and the stagnation of the past, and envisage a better future for animals and people, and a landscape of such rich biodiversity that we can only now dream.

In 2016 only three pairs of hen harriers successfully nested in England. There should be more than three hundred. The hen harrier has become a symbol of mismanagement of our uplands, yet it is also a symbol of hope for the future. With growing scientific knowledge about the impact of upland management, the successes of re-wilding in many countries, and the groundswell of support for hen harriers inspired by a campaign led by environmentalists Mark Avery and Chris Packham, I hope that the dream of rewilding our landscape, and rewilding our own lives, becomes a reality.

Gill Lewis

HEN HARRIER FACTS

Latin name: Circus cyaneus

Members of the hawk and eagle family, known as Accipitridae.

Males are a pale blue-grey with a white underside and black wing tips.

Females and young hen harriers are dark brown above with brown streaked breasts; they have a white rump and dark banding around the tail.

Hen harriers mostly make their nests on the ground amongst vegetation. The female needs to be well camouflaged, as she and her chicks are vulnerable to predators whilst in the nest.

As with most birds of prey, the female is larger than the male, weighing on average 530g compared to 350g for adult males.

Unlike other hawks and eagles, hen harriers have a round face, giving them an owl-like appearance.

Their owl-like faces are due to stiff facial feathers that direct the sound toward the ears, helping them to detect small mammals and birds concealed in vegetation.

Hen harriers have an impressive wing span, which extends up to 109cm in males and 122cm in females. However, despite their size they are relatively light birds, allowing for elegant and masterful flight manoeuvres.

They forage on the wing, flying close to the ground, with their wings held in a V-shape, gliding low in search of prey.

They feed on small birds and mammals, mainly pipits and voles.

Their diet can include red grouse, which brings them into conflict with gamekeepers on driven grouse moors.

During the mating season, males perform an acrobatic flight display to attract females, a practise that lead to the birds being nicknamed Sky Dancers.

During a sky dance, males will soar up to dizzying heights before suddenly plummeting towards the ground in a series of impressive twists, tumbles, and turns, pulling up just before impact with the ground.

Although hen harriers are protected by law, ongoing persecution and habitat loss is a constant threat to their survival.

ACKNOWLEDGEMENTS

This book could not have been possible without the help and generous time given by many people.

The issues surrounding driven grouse shooting have created heated arguments between those who want the sport to continue, and those who want to see a complete ban. I sought opinions and advice from people from both sides of the debate and thank them for their open and frank observations and discussions. It was from one such discussion that inspired me to write Joe, a gamekeeper's son, as the main character.

I would especially like to thank Dr Pat Thompson (RSPB Senior Policy Officer) and Dr Ruth Tingay, (raptor conservationist) for generously giving their time to read the draft manuscript. Their wealth of experience, knowledge and expertise was invaluable for providing answers to my questions about technical details in the story.

Thanks as always to my wonderful editor, Liz Cross, and the amazing team at OUP Children's Books.

Thanks to Ned who accompanied me on my travels with unbounded enthusiasm.

My research has taken me to the moors and introduced me to many books and peer reviewed scientific papers. I have followed online forums, news stories and the parliamentary debate about driven grouse shooting.

Key literature that has inspired much of the story includes;

The Hen Harrier by Donald Watson. A warmly written lifetime's study of the hen harrier accompanied by Watson's wonderful illustrations.

The writing and lectures of Frank Fraser Darling (1903-1979), an eminent ecologist who described the Scottish Highlands as devastated landscapes. He recognised that the devastation was a result of centuries of bad land use through deforestation, burning, and over-grazing. Significantly, he said that any policies that ignored this fact, could not hope to achieve rehabilitation of the land.

Georgie Monbiot's book *Feral* shines a light on the history of our landscape, how it has changed, and what could be achieved to increase biodiversity through allowing native habitats to reestablish (rewilding).

Mark Avery's book *Inglorious* scrutinizes the driven grouse shooting industry and the impact it has upon the people of both the rural and urban communities, the wild animals and habitats of the uplands. It highlights the continued persecution of birds of prey, specifically the hen harrier.

Websites of interest:

The RSPB Sky Dancer Project
https://www.rspb.org.uk/our-work/conservation/
conservation-projects/skydancer/

The Woodland Trust
https://www.woodlandtrust.org.uk

The Wildlife Trusts
http://www.wildlifetrusts.org

Rewilding Britain
http://www.rewildingbritain.org.uk

Raptor Persecution UK
https://raptorpersecutionscotland.wordpress.com

Become an RSPB Hen Harrier Hero today

Download your free activity pack to learn more about these spectacular sky dancers and help us spread the word to make sure there's always a home for hen harriers in our hills.

Complete six activities to become a Hen Harrier Hero, or ten to become a Superhero. Which will you be?

rspb.org.uk/henharrierhero

The RSPB is the country's largest nature conservation charity, inspiring everyone to give nature a home.

Illustration credit: Anthony Rule

Gill Lewis spent much of her childhood in the garden where she ran a small zoo and a veterinary hospital for creepy-crawlies, mice, and birds. When she grew up she became a real vet and travelled from the Arctic to Africa in search of interesting animals and places.

Gill now writes books for children. Her first four novels, *Sky Hawk, White Dolphin, Moon Bear,* and *Scarlet Ibis* published to worldwide critical acclaim and have been translated into many languages.

She lives in the depths of Somerset with her husband and three children and writes from a tree house in the company of squirrels.

Sky Hawk

GILL LEWIS

'Opens your eyes, touches your heart, and is so
engaging it almost turns the pages for you.'
Michael Morpurgo

Something lives deep within the forest . . .
something that has not been seen on Callum's farm for
over a hundred years. Callum and Iona make a promise
to keep their amazing discovery secret, but can they
keep it safe from harm? The pact they make will change
lives forever.

GILL LEWIS

BEST-SELLING AUTHOR OF *Sky Hawk*

'A beautifully told, nail-biting tale,
that will inspire and
empower anyone who reads it.'
Kate Humble

White Dolphin

When they first meet, Kara and Felix can't stand each
other. But on discovering an injured dolphin calf on
the beach they know they must work together to save
it. Now friends, they set out to find the truth behind
the disappearance of Kara's mother, and to protect the
nearby reef. But powerful people don't want them to
succeed. And with the odds stacked against them, how
can Kara and Felix make their voices heard?

GILL LEWIS

BEST-SELLING AUTHOR OF *Sky Hawk* and *White Dolphin*

Moon Bear

A boy and his bear, both longing to be free . . .

When twelve-year-old Tam is sent to work at a bear farm in the city, he has never felt so alone. He hates seeing the cruel way the bears are treated, but speaking up will mean losing his job. And if he can't send money home, how will his family survive? When a sick cub arrives at the farm, Tam secretly nurses it back to health and they develop an unbreakable bond. Tam swears to return his beloved cub to the wild, but how will they ever find a way to be free?

GILL LEWIS

THE BEST-SELLING AUTHOR OF *SKY HAWK*

Scarlet Ibis

Whatever it takes,
I must get my brother back . . .

Scarlet's used to looking after her brother, Red. He's special—different. Every night she tells him his favourite story—about the day they'll fly far away to the Caroni Swamp in Trinidad, where thousands of birds fill the sky. But when Scarlet and Red are split up and sent to live with different foster families, Scarlet knows she's got to do whatever it takes to get her brother back . . .

GILL LEWIS
THE BEST-SELLING AUTHOR OF SKY HAWK

Gorilla Dawn

A new day. A new dawn. A new chance.

Deep in the heart of the African jungle, a baby gorilla is captured by a group of rebel soldiers. Imara and Bobo are two children also imprisoned in the rebels' camp. When they learn that the gorilla is destined to be sold into captivity, they swear to return it to the wild before it's too late. But the consequences of getting caught are too terrible to think about. Will the bond between the gorilla and the children give them the courage they need to escape?

Here are some other stories we think you'll love ...

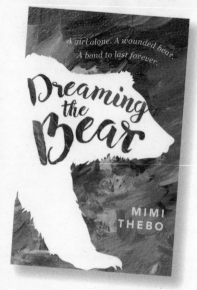

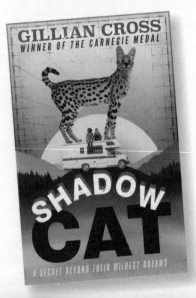